Glassheart

KATHARINE ORTON

WALKER
BOOKS

First published 2020 by Walker Books Ltd
87 Vauxhall Walk, London SE11 5HJ

2 4 6 8 10 9 7 5 3 1

Text © 2020 Katharine Orton
Cover artwork © 2020 Sandra Dieckmann

This book has been typeset in Sabon and Tisdall

Printed and bound by CPI Group (UK) Ltd, Croydon CR0 4YY

British Library Cataloguing in Publication Data:
a catalogue record for this book is available from the British Library

ISBN 978-1-4063-8523-6

www.walker.co.uk

MIX
Paper from
responsible sources
FSC
www.fsc.org   FSC® C020471

For Nan Axon

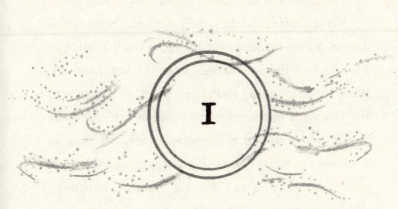

I

IN THE COLD, STILL HOURS OF NIGHT, WHEN
shadows swathed the wildwoods and most people
were in bed, footsteps creaked on the landing near
Nona's door. She froze at her desk – pencil poised
over her sketchbook, heart in mouth. Her wide, dark
eyes glittered by the light of a faltering candle. This
was what she'd been waiting for. The reason she'd
stayed awake all this time. Yet the sound still chilled
her blood. She held her breath. Listened.

A fox shrieked from the Wiltshire wilds beyond
her window – its cry so human and eerie that it made
Nona's skin prickle. There'd been foxes in London
where she was born and had lived, of course, but
there they were more likely to rattle the dustbins than
to howl in that terrible, mournful way. That's not
what she was listening for, though.

The floorboards creaked again. Closer this time.

Nona snuffed out the candle with quick fingertips. The wick hissed and sent up the sharp smell of sulphur. Putting out lights was ingrained in her from the Blitz. It had been her task, aged seven, to run around the flat with her brother, plunging it into darkness at the first notes of the air-raid siren; the hum of a bomber's engine. Even in the years since the war ended, dimming lights whenever she heard something strange or out of place was more of a reflex than ever. Now it included any sudden sound – the backfire of a motorbike; yelling voices.

Or footsteps.

The candle's glow had brought out the gold in Nona's wild brown hair. Now the moonlight picked out the silver of the slim scar that ran down the length of one cheek.

A slender shadow slipped under the crack below her bedroom door. It grew bigger. Sliding across the unvarnished boards from one side to the other. *Uncle Antoni, is that you?* she wanted to call out. But the words stuck fast in her throat, frozen there. She was almost certain it was him. *Almost.* And yet the tread sounded different somehow. Heavier. What if it was an intruder, come to rob their downstairs workshop? A shiver ran through her at the thought. The lead and solder they kept down there, for the making of stained-glass windows, would fetch a good price on the black market.

Nona decided it was best to stay quiet. If she called out and it was Uncle Antoni, she might never discover why he'd been creeping around in the night so often lately.

The shadow withdrew across Nona's floor and the footsteps passed her room, heading towards the stairs. That meant the person must have come from Uncle's room just across the landing. So it had to be him. Didn't it? She channelled a slow, deep breath to calm her nerves. Besides, why would a thief be up *here*, where the lead and solder wasn't?

Nona tucked the pencil behind one ear, eased herself silently out of her chair and snuck towards the door. She was quick and light on her feet and knew where to tread to avoid making a noise. Of all the kids from her old building, she'd been the best at tag whenever they'd played it on the common. Practically unbeatable – aside from her brother, of course. But that cramped building in London, and all those kids, were gone now. Everyone was. Except for Nona.

Once at her bedroom door, Nona timed the opening of it with the steady thud and creak of footfall. She peered into the dimly lit hallway. Moonlight shone through the small, curtainless window above the stairs, made from a hotchpotch of glass offcuts. It cast the bare floorboards in reds, blues and greens. Even though Uncle Antoni had thrown it together from scraps, it was still beautiful. As if he couldn't help but be a master craftsman, even when using the broken bits that other people threw away.

The light shifted. A figure slid beneath the colours. The sudden movement lodged the seed of a cry in Nona's throat, but it was Uncle all right. The rich shades glided over his skin, his clothes, before he came out the other side just at the foot of the stairs. He turned a corner, and was out of sight.

Even from the way he walked, all hunched over, Nona could tell he wasn't his usual, breezy self. He could only be in the grip of a dream … couldn't he?

For as long as Nona had lived with Uncle Antoni, he'd been a terrible sleeper. It was the only time he talked about the war: during nightmares in sleep-laced Polish – his mother tongue – that were loud enough to wake Nona from her own. He'd been known to sleepwalk too, in his bumbling kind of way. Once she'd caught him downstairs in his nightgown, trying to eat a candle. She'd taken it out of his hands and sent him back upstairs to bed. But this? It wasn't the same. He strode with a purpose. A direction.

As if he'd been called – and had no choice but to go.

The thought made her skin prickle. The night before last she was sure she'd heard him speaking to someone. But they lived alone. Just him and Nona.

Her heart pounded as she edged onto the landing. She couldn't get left behind. She couldn't risk him seeing her either. If he did she might never find out what was going on. "Here we go, then," she said to herself, rubbing the goose pimpled skin of one arm. She started down the stairs, treading in unusual places on the boards in the hope of avoiding the creaky spots.

The darkness deepened at the foot of the stairs. The sharp, warm smell of linseed oil flooded Nona's senses. Everything smelled of the thick, golden oil down here, because it was the main ingredient in the cement for their stained-glass window making, to keep the mixture nice and runny. It was one of those scents that seeped into everything and lingered – even and especially on a person's skin.

Outside the wind picked up – moaning through the nearby woods and causing thuds and whistles in the old, draughty house. A flood of coolness stroked the back of Nona's neck as she squinted into the dark, but her eyes hadn't adjusted yet. She couldn't see her uncle now. At all.

Until a lamp flicked on in the tiny, cluttered

painting room – a dozen paces across the length of the workshop. Her uncle was inside it. Already. Any minute he would shut the door. Then Nona wouldn't find out what he was up to.

"Nooo. No, no, no," she moaned to herself. She'd never make it in time.

Nona set her jaw. She wasn't about to give up yet.

Keeping close to the wall, she made a dash through the dark, straight for the tiny room. The wind moaned again – and the house whistled as if in reply – the sounds flooding her ears as she sprinted. Uncle Antoni shuffled away from the desk lamp he'd lit and turned towards the door. Towards her. She froze on tiptoes, bent at the waist, her arms thrust out for balance. But he stared straight through her, unseeing, and pushed the door slowly to. Nona let out her breath and surged forwards again. The door was closing. The light from inside was soon nothing more than a sliver. Nona reached it the second the light winked out.

She clawed at the jamb but it slipped out of her fingers. The last segment slotted into its frame with a clunk. The key turned in the lock. That was that. She was too late.

Nona clenched her fists and threw back her head in a silent howl of frustration. Then she crouched down, hugged her knees and thought. She tried not to focus on the darkness around her. Or how frightening Uncle's blank expression had been, how ill – almost trancelike – he'd looked. Or the fact that, if anything happened to him, she'd be completely alone again.

He was the only one who would take her in after the bomb destroyed her home and everyone in it. People in the village had grown tired of giving homes to dirt-ridden children from London by then, what with the earlier wave of evacuees. But Antoni Pilecki did. Perhaps it was his need for an apprentice that had driven him to take in the seven-year-old, as he'd casually told the nosier villagers. Or maybe the real truth was because he knew what it was like to be somewhere new and among strangers. Or because he too had lost everything in the war. His family. His homeland. Later, his ability to fight, when his injury put him out of the air force for good.

They weren't related, but it didn't matter. There is companionship in loss, and theirs made them as good as family. Nona was eleven now – they'd been inseparable for the last four years. And if Antoni ever decided to return to Poland? Then they would go together, no question. Although that was unlikely, Nona knew. The country had been carved up by the victors of the war: Poland's own allies, including

Britain. A betrayal Nona knew by the twist of his lips any time it came up that he felt bitterly. She could read him now, from the smallest flinch to the ghost of a wink – just as he could read her.

Beyond the door came more shuffling: her uncle moving around. And then his voice – usually warm and calm, now low and dark. Mumbled. Yet apparently in conversation. "Of course. We leave as soon as possible," she managed to catch. The rest was too hard to hear.

Nona's stomach flipped. Who could he possibly be speaking to? There wasn't another soul who lived in the house.

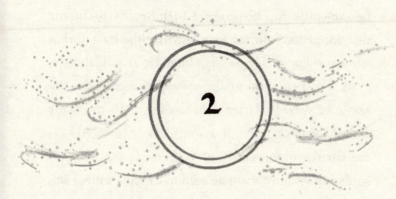

2

DID UNCLE ANTONI HAVE A TELEPHONE IN THERE, one that Nona didn't know about? Or a wireless?

With one ear pressed against the thick wooden door, Nona listened in. Still she couldn't make out what he was saying. Wait. Was that another voice replying to Uncle Antoni? A woman's, soft, smooth and singsong? Nona shuddered. There was something unusual – almost hypnotic – about that other voice. It came in waves – first near, then far. If only she could hear what they were saying. Or at least see inside...

Nona felt her way around the door and found the keyhole. The key blocked it from the other side, but it had a halo of light around it. The lock was old and loose. Perhaps she could nudge the key out somehow and get a glimpse of what was going on...

The pencil she'd tucked behind her ear could be the answer. There ought to be room to fit the sharpened end into the lock and give the butt of that key a good poke. Deftly, she slipped it in and jabbed – hard. The pencil tip made a snapping noise, but the key gave way. It clattered to the floor, on the other side of the door.

The voices stopped.

Nona withdrew the pencil quickly and bit her lip. She had two instincts, both forged in the Blitz: to run, and to hide. Right now she wanted to do both. She hesitated – pulled in opposite directions by curiosity and fear. Seconds passed. No one came to the door. Perhaps – *perhaps* – she'd got away with it.

Guilt twanged inside her. Should she even be listening in at all? This was clearly something Uncle wanted to keep private. There were few things he wouldn't tell her if she asked – and he usually had a good reason when he didn't. Maybe she ought to just trust him this time, as normal?

No. It had gone on long enough. Working on plans in secret. Talking behind locked doors. Not drinking his tea. Nona was his apprentice. She did his paperwork. No job ought to be kept secret from her. He never locked doors. And he always – *always* – drank his tea…

Nona peered through the lock with one eye – and bit her lip so she didn't yell with triumph. Her plan had worked. With a bit of shifting from side to side, Nona could see most of the room.

Her uncle and the other voice mumbled to one another again – more quietly this time. Nona saw Uncle Antoni, surrounded by shelves cluttered with brushes and powdered paints. Perfect faces rendered on pieces of glass stared back at her from the angled painting table in various stages of completion: Uncle's work, and none in the world more beautiful. It wasn't just Nona who thought so either. People sought his skill from all over the country, to restore church windows destroyed in the war. That's what they did now – together.

The illustrated eyes glittered in such a lifelike way it made Nona feel watched. The back of her neck prickled. But besides her uncle and those painted stares, there was no one else to be seen. No telephone or wireless either. Nothing that could have made the sound of that other voice. She strained to see every corner of the room. Surely the owner of the voice must be somewhere, made by something…

A movement at the corner of Nona's eye drew her attention back to the glass faces. She'd been wrong, she realized. Not all of them were painted on. One of them shifted, moved. It was a *reflection*. Of a woman with honey-coloured hair. A woman who wasn't there. Nona's whole body turned icy cold. She scanned the room again wildly. It wasn't possible – there had to be someone making that reflection. But there wasn't.

Nona's stomach turned. Everything inside her screamed that she was being watched.

With dread, Nona's eye returned to the reflection. The woman stared out of the glass, straight at her – as if she could see Nona through the solid wood door – and smiled. Her eyes gleamed. For long seconds, Nona couldn't move or breathe. She could barely do anything except stare back into those eyes.

Then the woman tipped her head and moved. A curl of hair, an embroidered sleeve, flashed across each of the glass pieces. She *had* to be coming for the door.

Nona turned on her heel and pelted for the stairs. She rushed up them, no longer worried about being heard. When she got to the landing, she dived through her bedroom door and shut it tight.

She sat with her back against the door, panting. Her head thrummed with dizzying blood. It couldn't have been real. It just *couldn't*.

Then again, it was hardly the first time she'd seen things that others didn't. People who were there one minute and disappeared the next. Animals with human-looking eyes that stopped to watch her. Strange trails of lights glinting in the woods at the back of their home, like pinpricks of dancing dust weaving through the trees – as if leading somewhere. Yet they would usually end at stones or trees and go no further. She didn't dwell on any of this – and she certainly never told anyone. It wouldn't do to admit these things. She knew that. How the village gossips would use such information didn't bear thinking about. They saw her as an outsider as it was.

Nona waited: until Uncle's footsteps – still oddly heavy – clumped across the landing, pausing outside Nona's door. She held her breath, watching his shifting shadow on the floorboards around her. Would he come in? Laugh, and explain it was all a big misunderstanding? Instead his shadow slipped away. Uncle carried on to his room.

There his to-ing and fro-ing reverberated through the walls, joining with the other sounds of the house: the creaks, the whistle of draughts. Would he ever go to sleep? And could the strange woman still be there, lurking around downstairs?

What stuck in Nona's mind was how familiar the woman had looked. And the way she'd smiled at Nona through the door … it was as if she knew her. Who was she? The questions swirled inside Nona like a whirlwind. An image flashed through her panicked mind, just as it always did when she was overwhelmed: her old home in London. A thousand glass shards frozen in the air around her, glinting like jewels. Their curtains in shreds. That feeling, that she was inside a box about to be crushed. The smell of burning.

It was her one and only memory of the night the bomb hit. She'd relived it a hundred times. She couldn't stand to relive it again now.

Nona leaped up and crossed the floor. She snatched a small object from its usual place propped against her windowpane and clutched it to her chest. Soon, the thundering of her pulse, her breathing, began to slow, and she opened her hands to peek at the object.

Inside was a piece of rounded, pinkish-red glass. Typical, Nona thought, that some children would have a doll or a teddy for comfort, while she had this. A half-heart in shape, its edges were smoothed with age, its one sharp point filed off for her by Uncle Antoni. It was thick in some places, thinner in others, which Nona knew meant it was likely to have been hand-rolled rather than made by machine. That and its colour made it even more special. Pink and red glass got its colour from the most precious metal of all: gold.

But this piece was dear to Nona for another reason. It had once been a part of her old home – fixed into a Victorian upper window panel. She used to love how its glow would track across the room as the sun crossed the sky each day, falling first across the tablecloth, then the armchair, settling on her mother's face.

Everything else had been destroyed. Everyone killed – including her mother and brother. But that's what you could expect from a direct hit in an air raid. It was a miracle Nona had survived at all. In fact, no one could really explain how.

This piece of glass had been in her hand when the wardens came. In her shock she must have picked it up, though she had no recollection of doing that. Or of any of it at all.

Even now, the details were hazy. The doctor who'd put the stitches in the cut on her cheek had called it "shock". Muttered that her memories would return in time, and she'd likely wish they hadn't. But they never had.

Nona turned the piece of glass over in her hands, felt its half-heart shape, rubbed its cool surface with her thumb. She wished she understood why all this had brought her right back to that night in the Blitz.

Although the sharp edges of most glass filled

Nona with terror, this piece never failed to soothe her. Tiredness washed over her as she turned it. At a certain angle you could see a tiny crack inside the glass. One that hadn't yet reached the edges, but was a weakness nonetheless. It would eventually break the piece in two, Nona knew. The more she turned it, the warmer it felt, and the more that warmth moved through her fingers and up into her bones. When she closed her eyes she could see its reddish-pink glow on the inside of her eyelids, as if standing once again under its light.

From the glow emerged shapes. Images. The woman she'd seen in Uncle's painting room – the way she'd looked right at Nona and smiled. A glimpse of a long road, and trees rushing past. Then a great expanse of wild, rolling land. A flash of something dark beyond it that made her momentarily catch her breath.

It wasn't unusual for Nona to see things when she held the glass. In fact, she'd come to expect it. With the half-heart still clutched in her hand, Nona's exhausted mind crossed over the threshold into sleep, carrying the visions with it. There she saw the woman again, inside an unfamiliar place: a temple perhaps, or a church.

And there was something else. *Someone* else. Like sensing the weather turn, Nona felt her dreams grow thick and heavy with threat. Though she fought against it, her mind was drawn out into the wilds, onto the rolling hills she'd seen earlier. A chilling darkness gathered like storm clouds, wrapping itself around a figure. A man, it looked like, but with a stag's head – whom she could just make out on the horizon.

3

NONA WOKE TO FIND UNCLE ANTONI SHAKING HER,
his face drawn. Light flooded the room, though dark
shadows clung beneath her uncle's wide eyes. Silent
fright bled into every part of Nona's body. This was
Uncle, no one to be afraid of. But by the look on his
face something must be drastically wrong. Nona
reached out and gripped his arms tight.

"Uncle! What is it?"

As soon as she met his gaze his shoulders relaxed.
"We have to leave," he said. His voice was calm – it
didn't match his eyes. Had he slept at all? What time
was it?

"What?" gasped Nona. "Leave? To go where?"
She looked all around. *"Now?"* Judging by the
light streaming through the windows she must have
seriously overslept.

Uncle nodded. Nona's heart sank. She didn't want to go anywhere – all journeys put Nona on edge, raised bad memories – yet there was no question of her staying here without him. Wherever one of them went, so did the other. It was their pact.

"We've got some windows to install for a job, Jenny Wren," he replied simply. "In Dartmoor. It'll just be a short trip." Jenny Wren was what he often called her, even though her name was Nona – because, he said, she was small, fast and worked hard, like the bird.

"How long?" Nona asked, bemused. But he just told her to pack a bag with clothes and anything she might need for a short stay, then stood and left the room without another word.

Nona was stunned. Was this something to do with the woman from last night? She'd heard Uncle talk about leaving as soon as possible. But what, exactly, had she seen? A woman who wasn't there – who had no doubt been the one who'd spoken to her uncle in soft, hypnotic murmurs. And then there'd been her nightmares... Nona picked up the half-heart where it had fallen into her lap. She should've known better than to sleep near it. Doing so always gave her the strangest dreams. Though she hadn't expected anything quite as strange – and frightening – as the stag-headed man.

Nona did as her uncle had asked and packed some

things – including the half-heart. It was a little piece of home – of comfort – which she wrapped in hankies and tucked safely in her pocket.

Her head thumped as she stepped out into the slicing air and towards the van where Uncle waited. It was packed full of glass and window-making materials. For an instant she hesitated, desperate to stay. Yet she couldn't – not after what she'd seen last night. She'd never feel safe, even if she was allowed to stay in the house alone. Which she wasn't. And what of their pact?

From somewhere nearby an owl up late shrieked a warning cry, sending chills through her. Nona climbed into the van, and they set off.

Far beyond the tangle of trees that lined the winding road, Nona caught a glimpse of moorland. She drank it in through the passenger seat window: the delicious ebb and flow and roll of the landscape, the distant dips brim full with mist. The sight should have filled her with wonder. Yet all she could feel was dread. Hadn't she seen glimpses of this last night – in her muddled dreams? Would she see the woman again too? And what about that stag-headed figure – the one wearing storm clouds like a cloak? The thought of it chilled Nona's bones.

They travelled in silence for hours. Down the country lanes of Wiltshire and out onto the grey stretch of endless roadways that had brought them to where they were now: an unfamiliar landscape that grew wilder and more ragged by the second. It had been afternoon already by the time Uncle woke her – her late night must have taken its toll – and the day felt like it was racing away from her untethered. Around her, everything felt like it was closing in: the narrowing road. The looming trees. The heavy sky.

A flash of something caught her eye on the horizon: the dark shape of a man. She whipped round to look closer. Instead Nona caught her own reflection in the window of the van, and hid from it instinctively behind her hair – allowing the brown strands to fall across her cheeks, her scar. She hated to see it because it reminded her of the way others always stared. She scowled in frustration. It wasn't all there was to her, yet it was all so many people cared to see.

Still, the odd silhouette she thought she'd glimpsed wasn't there. Her skin prickled. There was that feeling again from last night: of being watched.

Worse, since last night's events, Uncle's strange behaviour was getting stranger. Should she ask him about what she'd seen last night, straight out? Could she? It would mean admitting to spying on him. Nona felt like she would explode unless she confronted him about the reflection in the glass. But his strange, brooding silence – so unlike him – unnerved her. So she kept quiet.

Nona squeezed her coat pocket, to remind herself of the half-heart glass inside. She studied Uncle Antoni. He looked vacant, hunched over the wheel, his eyes drilling ahead as if all he could think about was their destination. A stab of panic left her heart thumping. What if he got worse out here in the middle of nowhere and she needed to find help? He was the only person Nona had left in the world. If anything happened to him...

"Uncle?" Nona tested. Her voice came out hoarse and quiet. When he didn't respond she spoke up. *"Uncle?"*

This time he gave a start. "Yes, Jenny Wren?" Though he smiled, his eyes bulged when he glanced at her, like someone who'd woken far too early from sleep.

"Where exactly are we going again?" Nona said, relieved that he'd at least replied.

"Oh, you know... A place in..." He gestured one-handed to their surroundings but couldn't seem to keep his train of thought going.

"Dartmoor?"

"Yes! Precisely." Uncle Antoni hesitated before

he went on, and when he spoke he did it slowly, as if the words were hard to form. The details difficult to remember. "It's a small village. Abandoned, as far as I know. The church was hit during the war by a German plane that went off course. Looking for Plymouth, I think."

This was progress. Now to see if Nona could keep him talking. Bring back a little of the Uncle Antoni she knew, and get a proper grip on their situation. "Dartmoor is huge, Uncle," she said. "I don't want us to get lost, and sunset's not far off. Maybe if you show me on the map..." They went over a rise in the road too fast. Nona's stomach lurched. The sheets of glass, stacked and secured with leather straps in the back of the van, slammed against the side. The thought of glass smashing terrified her. It reminded her too much of the Blitz. Of that night.

"Uncle?" she said when he still didn't reply.

"Hmm?"

"The map?"

Uncle Antoni scowled. "What does it matter where we're going?" he snapped. "Just trust me, will you? You don't need to know every little thing."

Heat rose in the back of Nona's neck, and her eyes prickled. He never usually kept secrets from her. The only thing her uncle refused to talk about was the war, besides the bare basics. His escape from Poland after it was invaded, then his time in the Royal Air Force before his injury; the shrapnel that buried itself dangerously close to his spine. Even though, going on his medals, he was a war hero. *It's in the past*, he'd say. *Best left there.*

He said the same any time Nona tried to talk about what had happened to her too. Or how much she missed her mother, and her brother, Amos.

Was it in the past, though? Because most days Nona could feel the war's presence, hanging around her like thick, suffocating smoke. So much that she could smell its scent – of burning. Unease swelled in Nona like bad weather. She had that feeling again of being watched, but it was worse: as if they were being stalked. Shadows moved in the distance, at the edges of her vision, but she refused to look. They would only disappear if she tried.

A flurry of rain landed against the windscreen. It made a sound like the drumming of bony fingers and sent her nerves rattling further. That woman she'd seen last night… Was she real? What did she have to do with all this?

"Nona?" She jumped at her uncle's voice, the warm touch of his hand on her shoulder. His scowl was gone, replaced with worry lines on his forehead.

"I'm sorry I got angry," he said. "It was uncalled for. You were only trying to help."

Nona sighed with relief. The strange look in his eyes was gone. This was the person she knew. He shook his head and brought his other hand back to the steering wheel. "I don't know what's the matter with me," he muttered. He sounded frustrated, but this time it was with himself. "Am I catching a cold or something, or is this just what it's like to get old?"

Nona chuckled – he was hardly old – but she studied him curiously. Didn't he remember anything about last night?

"Have I told you any of the legends of Dartmoor?" Uncle Antoni went on. Nona shook her head. She couldn't stop herself from smiling. His knowledge of folklore was almost as boundless as his knowledge of glass. "No, Uncle."

"What? Not even the one about the bottomless lake? Or the witch who sends mists to trick weary travellers? Or even the *haaairy* hands that appear on people's steering wheels to send them off the *rooooad*?" He reached over to tickle her with his calloused, lead-stained fingers. Nona shrieked with laughter and batted them away.

The van swerved on the damp, uneven road. Uncle Antoni grabbed the wheel to steady it. The brakes screeched and the wheels juddered, refusing to grip. They overcorrected and veered the other way. Nona's shoulder bashed against the side window as the glass sheets thumped and rattled in the back again. Uncle Antoni grappled with the wheel. The tyres gripped. Finally. Uncle Antoni managed to steer the van straight again.

Nona let out the breath she'd been holding in. She glanced at Uncle Antoni, wide-eyed, and he grimaced – part-relief, part-apology – before concentrating on driving.

The daylight was fading now, as Nona had predicted. And fast. The road was getting narrower still, bumpier, and deeper set inside the moors. The way ahead, and all around, had become concealed with bends and scrub, with more trees towering over them, crooked as the hands of fairy-tale crones, and with rotting, moss-covered walls to the sides. The rain was really coming down.

"Who's given us this job, Uncle?" This time, Nona hoped, she might actually get a proper answer out of him. Even so, her voice was quiet. Tentative. The dread had come back.

He scowled, and for one terrible second Nona thought he would snap at her again – but now it was confusion instead of anger. "Don't you know?"

"No! You haven't told me. Or shown me any of the paperwork. I keep asking, but—"

"*Really?*" He chuckled with an air of disbelief and shook his head. "I thought I'd left it all with you. Honestly. I feel all muddled, ever since... Ever since..." Nona could almost see the thoughts slipping away from him – sucked through the tiny open gap at the top of the driver's side window that made the air whistle past. It was the look in his eyes, growing ever distant. "Never matter," he said eventually.

"Who hired us, Uncle?" She couldn't keep the frustration out of her voice. But Uncle Antoni appeared not to hear her. He had his gaze fixed ahead again. Everything looked darker and glistened with the slick of rain: the trees, the drystone walls, the road. Some of the tall grass had been weighed down, bent and flattened against itself.

Desperation swelled in Nona's chest and burst out of her mouth before she could stop it. "Let's go back," she said. "This whole thing is wrong. Everything about it. Something's happened to you, something ... unnatural. If you need help, where will we go to get it, out here? What'll I do? I saw you last night, talking to that woman. Who is she? Has she got something to do with this? Tell me!"

Uncle Antoni didn't reply. He was gone from her

again, even though he sat right beside her. Nona chewed her lip and turned to the window so she didn't have to look at him. She tried to take deep, calming breaths. She had finally blurted out what was bothering her – only to be ignored.

Alongside them, where part of the wall fell away to nothing, Nona glimpsed a small cottage. Then another stone-walled home, further on, amid an endless sea of mist and moor, rising and falling. She felt miniscule. Overwhelmed.

Uncle Antoni slammed on the brakes. The force of it hurled them forwards, and then back into their seats again when the van stopped, dead. Nona had just enough time to glimpse the hare sitting tall in the middle of the road, its long ears pricked and its eyes trained on them, before it bounded away into the brush. It had looked straight at her, it seemed to Nona. As if it had been expecting them all along.

Only now did Nona spot the church up in front: a ruin with empty windows and half a sagging roof. Surely this wasn't the right place. It was a wreck! Far beyond anything that a set of new windows could do for it. Uncle Antoni slumped back in his seat, but still didn't take his eyes off the road. When he spoke, it was as if in a dream.

"We're here," he said.

4

"THIS CAN'T BE THE PLACE," SAID NONA. "IT'S NOT possible." She pushed open the door and walked to the centre of the dirt path, where the hare had sat staring at them with its strange, almost human expression. She'd seen animals with something uncanny about them before, but it was hard to explain what made them so. Like the hare, they almost looked as though they could speak if they really wanted to.

Nona stared around her and shuddered. The few houses dotted around were dark inside and shut up. A couple of them had been damaged and left to crumble. They must have been abandoned, like Uncle Antoni had said in the van. The whole place felt eerie and sad, somehow.

As for the tiny church – nature had clearly begun to reclaim it. Soft, furry moss carpeted the tiles on what was left of the roof, while ivy wove through gaps in the stonework and snaked up the walls. A sapling poked young branches through the naked, high-arched windows from inside. She didn't even have to go in to see that the place was derelict.

She fixed her uncle with a firm look. "There's no one here for miles," she said. "No one cares enough about this place to get it rebuilt. Look at it! It must be a mistake." He ignored her and opened up the back of the van, ready to start unloading. "Uncle!" she shouted. "Will you stop and listen to me?" She ran to him and grabbed his wrist, but gasped and quickly pulled away her hands. His skin felt deathly cold. The touch of it made her fingers tingle.

As if he hadn't heard her voice or felt her touch, he set about unstrapping the glass. He was in a kind of trance – just like last night. This was bad. He didn't respond to her, and now he was going to handle huge sheets of glass. And that ice-cold skin of his…

Nona hopped inside the back of the van and helped Uncle Antoni untie the straps. She swiped his safety gloves from their hook (where they usually stayed, unworn) and stuffed them quickly over his hands as best she could while he moved and worked. If she couldn't stop him, she'd just have to make sure he was safe.

When he grabbed several large glass sheets in one go and carried them towards the church, Nona couldn't help grimacing. She ought to help him, but she hated handling the glass itself. It was the thought – however unlikely, as long as she carried it safely – that at any moment it could break into shards in her hands. Glass had a personality of its own. Even Uncle Antoni would admit that. It could be unpredictable. You never knew what pressures had been working on it, from inside and out, that might make it suddenly crack.

At least Uncle Antoni's trance hadn't meant he'd forgotten how to hold it properly. Nona surveyed the sheer amount of supplies still crammed inside the van. Whoever the mysterious person was who'd brought them here, money was clearly no object. If they were being paid at all. It was all so strange.

Nona grabbed a toolbox and followed him to the door. But she dropped it in shock as soon as she stepped inside. From within, the building looked perfect. Where she'd expected the stench of mouldering leaves and damp, the smell of varnished cherrywood greeted her. Everything around her was beautifully carved in wood and stone: the pillars, the pews, the bench ends. Even the floor tiles were decorated in relief patterns of leaves and fruit.

The roof – which had looked like it was sagging in towards a great gaping hole from outside, was complete and supported with fresh, new beams. Although the sapling she'd seen from the outside was still there, growing close to a window in the middle of the church. The tiles were cut in a neat, deliberate circle around it.

Clearly this place had been refurbished, and very recently. All that was missing was the windows. And yet from the outside… Nona's back tingled. It couldn't be possible.

And there was something else. Something that made the walls feel to Nona like they were spinning. Because she'd glimpsed this place in last night's dreams – brought on by the half-heart glass.

She reached for it in her pocket – frightened all of a sudden that it might have fallen out and got lost – and felt a mite braver when her fingertips found it.

Light streamed in through the gaps where glass should be in shafts, leaving areas of deep, dense shadow. Eight of the arched spaces ran the length of the church – four on each side. And there was a grand window arch at the far end, where a raised altar stood.

What was that, over on the altar? There were stacks of pots and piles of what looked like blankets.

Nona picked up the tool kit again and carried

it over to where Uncle had started resting the glass against one wall, closer to the raised altar. It was food – tons of it. More fresh and potted items than she'd seen in one place in all her life. Fruit, bread, eggs, honey… Was this really for just the two of them? Her mouth started to water involuntarily. It would definitely beat the tins of spam she'd packed in their supplies. But even as she imagined the fresh tastes on her tongue a warning note rang in her ears. Could she really touch any of it without knowing who put it there, and why? Something mysterious was going on, and if there's one thing Nona knew it was not to take food when you didn't know where it'd come from.

Even more odd, perhaps, behind it all were soft-looking blankets and feather pillows, fit for about twenty people. Why was it all here?

Nona shook herself. She couldn't stand around staring. She had to help Uncle Antoni.

While he carried in the glass, Nona focused on the rest of their materials. Long wooden boxes filled with lead strips, called "came", some giant tubs of special cement that they would use to stop the glass from rattling inside the lead, as well as to keep out the elements, solder, tallow – and another heavy tool kit.

By now, Nona was damp with sweat. Her wavy hair stuck to her face in wiggly strings and her cheeks radiated heat. She couldn't imagine how Uncle must've felt after all that unloading. If things had been normal, they would've made a cup of tea on their portable Primus stove – hers with powdered milk, his black with a slice of lemon. Uncle Antoni would always insist on a tea break. He'd blame his injured back for the need to rest, and that was true ... but Nona knew that he enjoyed the artistry more than he did lugging around the materials. And she couldn't blame him for that.

Uncle Antoni didn't stop today, though. He unrolled one of the huge scrolls of paper he'd brought in, used for drawing out detailed plans called a "cartoon", and taped it to the largest window. He'd use charcoal to mark out its exact shape, so that when the stained-glass piece was assembled it would be certain to fit.

For a while, Nona watched him, wide-eyed. Was he ever going to stop? Panic swelled in her chest. Would he ever be himself again? What if the woman came back while he was like this? Without Uncle Nona felt seven again – small, lost and afraid.

"What's happened to you?" she said, slumping against the back of a pew, although this time she wasn't expecting a reply. She sighed deeply. Silver pinpricks of dust caught in the fading light from the windows billowed and scattered in her breath as if in a gale.

A resounding bang came from behind her.

Instinctively, Nona ducked behind the pew she'd been leaning against. Her heart pounded. She crouched absolutely still, curled up small with her knees pressed into her chest so that all she could take were tiny, rapid mouse breaths. Unwelcome memories flooded her mind. Of the times she'd done this before. Cowering in the crowded cellar of their communal building in London next to her brother, listening to the bombs fall.

The war is over, Nona told herself. *It's over.* She repeated it in her mind until she could finally bring herself to peek round the side of the bench. Still, as she did so, she felt sure in every bone of her body that she would see the devastated living room of her childhood. The aftermath of the night that had left her with her scar – and buried her family. The night no one made it to the cellar in time.

The war is over, she told herself again. Her fingers sought out the half-heart glass in her pocket.

The door was wide open, moving back slightly on its hinges. The sound must have been the door swinging open and hitting the wall, amplified by the large empty space. It wouldn't have needed a hard push to make such a loud noise. Had someone come in?

Nona could see little else around the bench but

the shafts of light from the windows picking out leaf patterns on the tiled floor. If she moved her head a little, she could also see the sapling. But no sign of an intruder. Perhaps the door had blown open in the wind?

A skittering sound tracked across the floor – as if someone had accidentally kicked a small stone. It came from the other end of the church, towards where Uncle Antoni still busied himself.

Someone was definitely here. They wouldn't see her, but what about her uncle? He'd be easy to sneak up on in his current state.

Nona wanted to spring from her hiding place and demand to know what this intruder wanted, fists clenched and ready to fight, if necessary. But she was rigid with fear – just as she had been all those years ago. The frozen snapshot of the moment the bomb hit rushed into her mind, clouding out everything else: the shattered glass of their living room windows hanging in the air. And she at the centre, surrounded... She saw it again now. Smelled the terrible burning smell that always came with it.

Something scuttled through the shadows, behind the sapling's trunk and near to the wall. Nona held her breath. What was that? A rat? Near to where she crouched, from the end of the pew, came a quiet chuckle.

Definitely not a rat.

Any closer, and whoever it was would see Nona. She had to do something before that happened. Could she frighten them off somehow?

She took a deep breath. It was now or never.

"Who's there?" she bellowed as loudly as she could. "Get out of here! You're trespassing." A sharp intake of breath, and then another scuttling sound. Something small darted through the shadows towards a stone arch that led to some stairs. Her shout, along with the surprise of seeing the creature, had released her from her petrification. Nona leaped to her feet. As she did so she caught sight of its back vanishing up the steps: a long tail with a forked end.

Not human. But not a rat either. Something else.

Shaking, Nona ran to the altar and grabbed a pestle and mortar – a shallow bowl and a long, hefty tool used for grinding herbs and spices. It was a good heavy stone one. In spite of her shout, Uncle Antoni hadn't even flinched from his window tracing. She left him, oblivious to the world it now seemed, and followed the creature to the foot of the stairs.

THE PESTLE AND MORTAR FELT COLD IN NONA'S hands. She gripped the pestle like a club, and hefted the mortar in the other, squeezing them both so tight that her fingers ached. The grey stone steps ahead of her were smooth and dipped with wear at the centre, the arched walls so narrow it felt like they might close in around her. Nothing but gloom lay beyond the archway high above.

She hesitated, afraid to take the first step.

"Who's there?" she called again, her neck prickling. Her voice echoed up the tunnel-like staircase and into the darkness beyond. No reply came. Adrenalin surged through her body and her heart pounded. She could hardly believe any of this was happening. She took the first step, and then the second. It seemed to get narrower the further in she went. Nona steadied herself on the cool stone and fought the urge to turn and run – to escape. "I'm coming up. I'm going to find you, so you might as well just show yourself!" she cried, more to give herself courage than anything. To fill that awful, waiting silence.

Still no reply. Could she have imagined what she'd seen and heard? The chuckle? The forked tail? Maybe it was just a rat, after all? The thought gave her enough courage to reach the final step.

Nona found herself on a tiny second floor. The whole church, second floor and all, was about the size of a large barn. All was quiet here – and still. Nona eased her grip on the pestle and mortar a little. Hearing Uncle Antoni, she could almost pretend things were normal. That he was working on a job as he normally would. But nothing was normal about any of this. Deep down she knew that.

The second floor was really just a balcony with room for a couple of rows of seats that would have run all the way around the walls. The space at the centre would have allowed anyone sitting up there to see the altar. There were some seats – wooden and beautifully carved – and, unusually, a couple of cosy-looking beds. Two beds – and two of them. Nona shuddered. It was normal for an employer to plan somewhere for them to stay. But were they guests here – or prisoners? It's not like they could leave with Uncle the way he was.

A movement disturbed the shadows. This time from under a seat ahead of her. Nona gripped the pestle and mortar so that her knuckles turned white and said again with a trembling voice, "Show yourself."

"*Craaw.*"

The sound was deep and gravelly. It had definitely come from under those seats. Nona strained her eyes. Waited. Something emerged from the gloom, fast – a creature, small and black and angular. It surged towards her in three rapid skips and cocked its head to eye her down its long, sharp beak.

A crow.

Nona would have been relieved. She would've written off the human chuckle, the forked tail, as her ears and eyes playing tricks on her. But something still didn't sit right. There was something different – special – about this bird. The way it looked at her. The way its eyes glinted at her... It looked unmistakably amused.

"Crows don't have forked tails," she said, ignoring the voice in her head that told her how ridiculous it was to be talking to a bird. Nona stared hard into its gleaming eyes to make the point that she was no push over, and that she didn't appreciate being mocked.

"And they don't laugh the way you did downstairs either," she added.

As if in response, the crow threw back its head and made a rasping sound in its throat – a strange, scratchy, strangled laugh, but not at all like the chuckle she'd heard.

A prickle of heat rose at the back of her neck. She was definitely being mocked now. But she wouldn't let it throw her off track: the way it had slunk in earlier and showed no surprise that Uncle was there made her think it had been sent to check up on them. By the mysterious woman, perhaps. "Come off it," Nona said, trembling. "That's not what I heard before." She raised the club-like pestle – and her voice. "Who are you, really? *What* are you? And what's happened to my uncle?" The last part came out in a long yell – one word bleeding into the next.

The crow leaped back from her in a flurry of feathers. It watched Nona for a second. Then, it parted its beak.

"All right, all right," came the strained bird-voice. "You've got me."

The crow tucked its head under its breastbone and rolled itself into a tight ball – one which shifted and wriggled and grew. Feathers became scales.

Wings became a second set of clawed feet. A long, forked tail rose out of the bundle.

Nona watched in horror as the crow transformed into something else. Except, when it lifted its head to look at her, she still wasn't sure what that something was. It looked like the kind of thing you'd see in a book of fairy tales – an illustration of an imp, or a demon. Nona's horror gave way to amazement. How could this be happening? Its scaly skin shimmered silvery grey, though its colour didn't seem fixed: it shifted from one second to the next, like a chameleon or a cuttlefish. Nona could do nothing except stare at the rippling colours.

The creature watched Nona for some time, and when Nona continued to gawp, it grinned, opened out its arms and said, "Ta-dah!"

Nona came back to herself sharply and shut her gaping mouth. The creature was still taunting her. And she was not impressed. Her cheeks burned.

"Don't you *Ta-dah* me." She lunged at it, brandishing the pestle. Her astonishment was long gone, and anger had seeded and quickly flourished. "I don't know what you've done to my uncle, but you'd better undo it. Right now!"

The creature put its hands in front of its face. "Wait. Don't hurt me. It wasn't *me* who put the spell on him."

Spell? The word struck panic into her heart, but she didn't let it show. "Who's done this to him, if it wasn't you? Tell me." Nona stamped her foot threateningly. The creature ducked and winced.

"Put that down and I'll tell you," the creature squeaked, nodding at the pestle.

Nona hesitated. She hadn't really intended to hurt the impish creature. She would only use the pestle to protect herself if it were to attack.

"Put it down," said the imp, more firmly this time. "Or I'll turn back into a crow and fly off, and you won't hear any more about the spell your uncle's under."

There was that word again: *spell*. Any other time Nona would've scoffed. But after everything she'd seen – Uncle's strange trance, the mysterious woman... And she *was* speaking to an imp, after all.

Nona's breath quickened, but she kept her fear and wonder hidden.

"Fine." She raised her eyebrows. "Then I'll break all the glass so he *can't* work." Nona knew how to play this sort of game. She'd had plenty of practice with her brother, and the other children who'd lived in their building. She was a master at upping the stakes. Making threats that were believable. The imp didn't have to know that she'd never smash the glass; that even the thought of it turned her stomach.

He'd already paled to something like the colour of ancient pearls. "That would make a mess of my place," he said, rubbing his chin.

Nona narrowed her eyes. "You live here?"

The creature just shrugged. "Do now," he mumbled. Something about its sudden casual tone made Nona lower her guard – enough to show a sliver of awe.

"Why does this place..." she began. "I mean, how—"

"—does it look abandoned from the outside but like this on the inside?" the creature butted in. Nona nodded. Curiosity distracted her from looking menacing now. Without noticing, she'd already lowered the hand that was holding the pestle.

"You really want to know?" The creature flashed her a wry smile, and then said, "It's to keep people like *you* away." He laughed. Nona scowled. "And," he went on quickly, "because it's currently in disguise. You can thank the spirits for that."

"Spirits?" Nona looked around her. Any belief in things like spirits or magic had been blown apart in the war. She'd spent every moment since distrusting her own eyes. The lights in the woods. The strange animals. The power of her glass piece, the half-heart, to give her uncanny dreams. But with everything that had happened in the past day, and in this place? How could she possibly deny it?

"That's right," the imp went on. "It's an umbrafell. Those are places that exist in two worlds at once. They're rare and special. That tree down there – see it? It's holding the spirit world and the human one together. Happens by chance and every umbrafell has a different power. Clever, eh?" Nona could feel his eyes on her as she stared around. "Not every human gets to see inside either," he went on. "You're lucky, you are."

Nona's attention snapped back to him. "Lucky?" she repeated, her tone sharp. Uncle Antoni being put under a spell and both of them being lured here didn't strike her as lucky.

As if sensing the need to change the subject, the creature reached its bulbous fingers towards Nona, offering a handshake. "I'm Castor, by the way."

"I'm Nona," she said, eyeing him warily. She stooped to place the mortar on the ground with the pestle safely inside it, and reached out to shake his hand. Castor's fingers felt cool and a little damp in hers. He grinned at her in the dusk light.

A loud clatter came from downstairs and echoed around the stone walls. Nona and Castor leaped apart, staring at each other with wide, startled eyes. She ran to the balcony and peered down. Uncle Antoni had dropped his tools and collapsed.

6

NONA RUSHED DOWN THE STONE STEPS TO HER uncle's side. "Uncle? Are you all right?" She clutched him round the shoulders.

To her relief, he groaned. "Ugh. I feel like someone's boxed me round the ears for several rounds. What's happened? Where am I?" He started and looked around, as if only just seeing his surroundings.

He'd heard her. And replied. Nona burst into tears and hugged him tight. Now it was Nona who could no longer respond, because she was too relieved to speak.

"Ah, my Jenny Wren. Nona. What's the matter? This isn't like you." Nona couldn't get the words out past her sobs. She gripped him even tighter, afraid to let go. It wasn't until he started to gently rub between her shoulder blades that she finally began to relax, and to feel able to speak again.

"I'm just so glad you're back, Uncle. We're in a church, somewhere in Dartmoor. You've been under a spell."

"A spell?" His voice caught in his throat, which sounded dry. He coughed. "I could believe it, the way I feel. Nona, I'm so parched. Let's have a brew on the Primus, eh?"

That was more like it. Nona leaped to her feet and helped heave him onto his. "Castor," she called, "could you grab the Primus from the van and—"

But Castor wasn't there. If he was still upstairs, he certainly wasn't showing himself.

With her uncle's arm across her shoulders, Nona helped direct him to a pew. "*Mój Boże*," he said, which Nona had come to learn meant "My God" in Polish. "This place is…" He'd been looking all around, but now his gaze lingered on the sapling growing through the middle of it all. "Unusual."

Nona laughed. "You should see it from the outside." She fetched water, got the Primus stove lit and made them both a cup of tea. As her uncle drank his, she raided some of the bread they'd brought, carved a wedge for them both, and coated it thinly with margarine – what she called "bread and scrape" – from their own supplies. This would be their evening tea. Although it was tempting to raid all the beautiful morsels just sitting there on the altar, she knew better than to go taking strange food. What if it was enchanted, and did something nasty to them? It looked too good to be true, so it was probably a trap.

"I feel like I should be helping," he said, watching her work. But Nona knew he was too weak to move, even if he'd wanted to.

"Don't worry, Uncle. You can slice all the bread you like for me when you're back on your feet." They both laughed.

Uncle Antoni ate and drank with shaking hands. Nona frowned as she looked around her. She'd need to sort out their beds soon. Uncle was exhausted. The ones she'd spotted upstairs would need extra blankets and pillows from the altar. It didn't feel as risky to take those as it did to eat the food. After all, a bed couldn't be enchanted … could it?

Their coming here had clearly been meticulously planned by someone – even down to where they would sleep. That wasn't odd in itself, although it was creepy that they hadn't been here to greet them, especially if they had nothing to hide. At least she wouldn't have to sleep on a pew though, which she knew from experience was no fun. While Uncle rested, Nona rummaged through the pillows and blankets, and selected some to drag upstairs.

"Craaw!"

Castor's crow voice echoed down the stone stairs as she made her way up.

"What is it?" she asked when she reached him. "And why are you hiding up here? My uncle's all right. He wouldn't try to hurt you or anything, if that's what you're worried about." Castor didn't answer, but instead scratched and scuffed at the ground with his claws. Did he not like to be seen as an imp? Was that why he'd changed, and hidden away? Or was he just not used to having people around? Perhaps it was a bit of both.

Nona made the beds. She was surprised that Castor helped her – sort of. A beak and claws weren't exactly great at bed-making.

Even though she'd left her uncle downstairs for a matter of minutes, Nona only had to take one look at him to know that his energy was fading fast. With his arm slung across her shoulders again, Nona helped him up the stairs.

By the time she'd lowered him onto the soft mattress, Uncle Antoni's eyes had already started to close. "I don't know what's happening to me, Jenny Wren," he said, squeezing her shoulder. "I am just so tired. I haven't felt this tired since … since…"

Nona squeezed his hand. "It's all right, Uncle.

You can rest now. But can you tell me anything about what happened to you first?" Nona bit her lip. She had one question that she really wanted to ask, though she was scared to in case the answer was no. If she didn't ask now the question would plague her.

"Could you hear me, when I was talking to you?" she said. "I mean, did you know I was there?" Something inside her shuddered at the thought that he might not have. Because if not it meant they'd been cut off from each other for the first time since they'd met. That both of them had been, in their ways, alone. She couldn't bear the thought.

Uncle Antoni didn't answer. His eyes were closed and he had started to snore.

"Looks like she's releasing him from the spell at night." Castor's voice close to Nona's side gave her a start. A quick glance showed her that he was an imp again. "That's something," he went on. "At least she's not planning to work him to death. You never know with spirits – they don't really understand how things are for the rest of us."

The rest of us? What did Castor mean by that? Was he not a spirit too? Nona blinked back the tears which were forming again at the memory of seeing her uncle so unlike himself.

"He'll be back under her spell come the morning, though," Castor added, not noticing the brief, curious glance Nona had given him. He sighed and began to hum.

Nona was still struggling to deal with all she'd learned that day. The whole ordeal. It felt like she'd been punched in the stomach. Suddenly it took a lot of effort just to breathe, and to swallow down the painful lump in her throat. When she could finally bring herself to speak, in a trembling voice, it was to say, "Take me to her. This witch or spirit, or whoever has done this to Uncle."

She turned to look at Castor properly for the first time since Uncle Antoni had fallen asleep. Her eyes were red-rimmed, she knew, but she couldn't help that – and she knew the heat in her cheeks would make her scar more visible. But at least she'd saved herself from actually crying in front of him. And, to Castor's credit, he hadn't looked twice at her scar. She would've noticed. She always did.

Castor shifted uncomfortably under her glare and turned a fleeting, sickly green. "Oh, that's not a good idea," he said. "And it's not like you'll be able to talk her out of it."

"I might."

"You won't."

Nona paused, and then said, "Tell her I'll smash the glass if she doesn't listen. And that if you hadn't agreed to take me to her I would've already. I don't care. I'll do it if I have to." Her stomach flipped at the words, but she really meant it this time. She'd do whatever it took to protect her uncle.

Castor swallowed hard and scratched behind his long, pointed ear with one of his clawed back legs. Nona watched, and waited. Castor went green again, flashed yellow, then went straight back to green. "Listen. Hey, come on… Stop that. Stop staring at me." He raked his sticky, fat-ended fingers down Nona's face, not unkindly, but not softly either. When he saw her renewed glare he jerked his hand away.

An apologetic smile became a wince. "Fine," he said eventually. "I'll tell you what. Get a bit of rest now, or whatever. Then before first light, I'll take you to see her. All right?"

A smile slipped across Nona's lips that she couldn't hide, even though she was trying to look stern. "Thank you," she said at last.

Castor flushed pink and studied the tiles. "That's *if* we can even find her, mind you," he grumbled. "She's good at hiding – never stays in one place for long. Might take us *for ever*. And I don't want you telling her that I agreed to this either. Make sure she thinks you forced me."

"I did force you."

"Well, then. That's fine."

Castor left her then, in search of his own dinner. Nona could only guess what a creature like him – imp, crow, or whatever he was – actually ate. But he promised he'd be back to wake her when it was time. And she had little choice but to trust him as he turned into a crow and flew off.

Only when Nona settled into the soft mattress that had been left for her did she realize how much she ached. How exhausted all the worrying had made her. It had been one strange surprise after another. In particular, nothing could have prepared her for this place. Everything in here was perfect, but from the outside its walls had seemed steeped in tragedy. She wondered if anyone had been inside it when the bomb fell. If anyone had survived.

She unwrapped the half-heart glass from her cloth hankies. Having it there was her biggest comfort. She'd seen so much with its help last night – the woman, the church, that strange figure on the horizon… Was it all connected? Nona didn't relish the idea of another disturbed night's sleep, but what if her glass helped her dream something important – something that might help her when she met the spirit tomorrow?

Nona wrapped it up again and placed it carefully beside her. With one hand resting on the half-heart and the woollen blanket around her, she closed her eyes. She tried to push all her worries away. It felt impossible. She was bundled up warm, but she couldn't stop shuddering. Every time she closed her eyes, an impression formed on the inside of her eyelids. A dark mass, rising tall. Forming itself into a shape with every dismissive blink.

The shape of a man.

Nona opened her eyes and shook the vision away. Why was she seeing that? She wasn't even asleep yet. The events of the day must have really got to her.

And tomorrow would be worse. Tomorrow she would face the one who'd bewitched her uncle.

7

NIGHTMARES PLAGUED NONA. THE VISION OF THE silhouetted man grew stronger – as if he was coming closer. She could see his stag horns more clearly now. At times she could even hear the howling winds that whipped around him, see the thunderous storm clouds swirling in the sky above his head. Nona's chest felt tight with fear – her body heavy and frozen. She didn't want to look, but couldn't look away. What she dreaded most, she realized, was that he would turn his gaze on *her*.

Nona couldn't see much besides his outline against the sky. But a strange, red glow emanated from his chest...

Only much later and for the briefest instant did her nightmares fade. She was a bird, then – a wren, like her uncle called her – swooping and diving and circling inside the church walls. Those walls... It was as if she could feel their magical, protective power. Her heart soared. And when she opened her mouth, a flood of joyous burbles and chirps came out.

Castor woke her. She leaped upright and glanced all around, her heart pounding almost as fast as it had when she'd dreamed of being a bird soaring up to the ceiling. "S'all right," said Castor. "It's only me." He was in his imp form and gave her a huge grin.

It was still dark. But even in the gloom Nona noticed the single, tiny feather on the pillow next to her hand: a wren's feather. It twirled in the stream of her warm breath.

It had all been a dream... Hadn't it?

Although it wasn't yet light, birds outside had begun their dawn chorus, and Uncle Antoni's bed was empty. He'd started working again – relentlessly. None of the usual yawns and chatter or strong cups of tea. He'd taken the paper roll down from the window already and started to transfer designs that he must've made in secret before they arrived on to it.

Nona's heart sank. She'd give anything to have Uncle back the way he was.

"Come on," said Castor. "If we're going to stand a chance of finding her we'd better set off." He screwed up his face. At first Nona thought he was pulling a weird expression. That perhaps he was in pain or had trapped wind. But then his face grew pointed and his eyes shrank to little black beads and she realized: he was transforming into a crow. Wings sprouted from his back, shot upright and opened out. His silvery scales plumped out and darkened to deepest, sleekest black.

He studied her down that long, jet beak, then hopped onto her shoulder, clumsily clouting her round the head with his wing as he did so. She scowled and rubbed her cheek. Castor threw back his head and did his eerie bird-laugh. It surprised Nona how strong the grip of his long, sharp claws felt. The jumper she'd slept in was already tatty from where the glass in their studio had caught and cut. It didn't need any more holes.

"*Craaw!*" Castor shrieked in her ear.

"Stop it! I'm moving." Nona took the hint and dragged herself slowly to her feet. After the disturbed night, just standing sent stabs of dagger-like pain through her temples. She slipped her half-heart glass into the pocket of her skirt.

"*Craaw!* What's that?"

Nona took it out again and unwrapped the hankies. "It's—"

She was about to explain when something glinted across its surface. Quickly she held it up to her face.

Two women walked together in the pink glass before fading into shadow near the stairs. One wore a golden shawl and had black hair streaked with silver. The other was the woman Nona had seen in her uncle's studio. She was certain of it.

"She's here already," hissed Nona. "Look!" But when she looked past the half-heart, she saw no one. Nona held it up again to peer through. Nothing. She ran to the stairs and Castor let out a surprised squawk. Still no one. Nona rubbed her forehead and stared at the glass. It had never *shown* her anything before – except in her head and in her dreams. But what exactly *had* it just shown her?

Castor flapped his wings, whipping up a breeze. "*Craaw*. Magic!" He cocked his head and hopped down the length of Nona's arm, pressing his eye up close to the glass. Weird noises came from his throat – odd groans and gurgles, as if he was working through his puzzlement. "I think, shows was," he said eventually. "*Was* here. Not now. Shows *was*."

So the glass could show her glimpses of the past? Is that what Castor meant? Was that what her strange dreams amounted to as well? That felt different, though – as if there was more to it when she dreamed or closed her eyes and had images pass through her mind. Like drawing from a store of energy that it had inside it. This had been just the briefest glimmer.

Castor folded his wings and hopped up to her shoulder again in lots of little jolts. "Hey!" she complained, until his feathers rustled close to her ear again.

"Take it," Castor added, quieter this time, bobbing his head towards the glass fragment in Nona's hand. "Will help. Show way."

Nona packed a rucksack with a flask of water, and her sketchbook and pencils which she took everywhere. Before leaving the church, Nona rested a hand on Uncle Antoni's ice-cold arm. "I'll be back, Uncle," she said softly. "I promise." She waited for the slightest response – a twitch of his arm muscle or a whispered word. None came. Nona sighed and headed into the dawn.

⤜⋙

The moors stretched out in front of Nona beneath a low-lying mist. February frost laced the grass at her feet and crunched underfoot. She could see it sparkling through the swell that stirred around her ankles and curled in the distance in slow waves. Under the sepia sky and lopsided moon, the mist looked like a pale sea carrying diamonds.

Nona shivered and rubbed her arms. "Where are we going?" she asked. Her breath floated away from her in a skyward river.

Castor parted his beak and squawked, "Don't need to know. Just go."

"Thanks for nothing," grumbled Nona. "I'll just keep walking this way, then, shall I? Why can't you turn back into ... whatever the *other* you is? And just explain—"

In response, Castor pecked her head – hard.

"Ouch!"

"Don't need to know. Just go."

"Fine." Nona rubbed the sore spot he'd made on her scalp. "Mind what you're doing with that beak," she said. "It's sharp."

They passed a lonely tree, its branches a dark tangle against the lightening sky. Nona glanced up as they went by. The vivid orange sunset eyes of an eagle owl met hers and watched her pass coolly. Nona shuddered and gripped the straps of her rucksack. "It feels like everything's watching me," she said.

Castor didn't reply.

A wink of golden light from the grass caught Nona's eye. And another beside it, hovering over a lump of quartz. Then a third beyond that, forming a string of lights, drifting slightly – just like the ones she sometimes saw in the fields and woods in Wiltshire.

"There," squawked Castor. "Going there." He seemed to be speaking about the lights.

"Castor," Nona tested, "do you see those lights too? What are they?"

Castor shuffled on her shoulder, as though surprised. Finally he said, "Spirit paths."

"Spirit paths!" Nona repeated. But what did that even mean? If she followed the lights would she eventually find the spirits? Usually they ended in an old tree or a rock when Nona had followed them before.

"Use the glass," came Castor's imp-voice beside her ear. "Let's see if she came this way. I'm not sure, but your glass should show us, I reckon. If it is what I think it is."

"What do you think it is?" asked Nona.

"Sometimes people see spirits through glass, and the first time it happens that piece of glass gets enchanted."

Nona frowned. She couldn't remember seeing anything *through* it until recently – just that it gave her strange dreams. And that she'd been clutching it after the night she lost her family. "But—" she began when a rustle on her shoulder told her he was changing back. Nona craned her neck to look at him but caught only the last of his scales becoming feathers. He'd transformed again. Why? What was he hiding from?

She knew she wouldn't get any answers out of him like this, however. She unwrapped her precious piece of glass and held it up to her face so that it caught the light.

Through it, she saw the two women from the church again. They walked beside the spirit lights and vanished as quickly as they'd appeared. The tiniest fragment of the past, caught inside Nona's glass. Nona marvelled at it. The shape. The uneven surface. The tiny bubbles frozen within. The crack inside that threatened to one day break it. She'd known it was special before – but this?

"They came this way," she said.

Castor only squawked, "Keep going!" and gave her hair an excited tug.

Nona followed the spirit path, every so often taking out her half-heart to check that the women had come this way. The path diverged in two. The glass showed that the women had parted there – the one with the golden shawl heading towards the woods, while the one with honey-coloured hair, the one from Uncle Antoni's studio, carried on across the moor. Nona followed *her* path. She had to be the one responsible for bewitching her uncle after all.

The strangest thing was that this felt familiar somehow. Had she dreamed it last night, in among the chaos of her other visions?

After what felt like an age of walking, Nona's legs and lungs ached. The chill in the air had lifted at least, and washed-out mounds of land peeked through the mist. Birds sang all around them – although Nona couldn't tell where any of them were. The sky had turned from brown to a murky blue-grey, but the moon hung in it as bright and silvery as ever.

The spirit path led to a group of trees standing tall on a rise of land. The grass turned from hardy tufts of pale straw to a soft, bright green carpet stretching out on a downward slope, glittering with ice in the half-light. The remnants of the mist had pooled inside a mossy stone circle. Nona glanced around. It was entirely concealed by the way the ground dipped. She'd never have known it was even there.

Something moved at the centre of the stone circle. An animal, perhaps? Looking closer, Nona couldn't see anything at all. Had she been mistaken?

"See there. There," cawed Castor, and gave Nona's hair another tug.

"Ow!" She pushed him away and gave her scalp a rub again. She peered through the half-heart glass. At the centre of the stone circle was a woman lying very still. *The* woman. This time she didn't fade away.

And, when Nona lowered the glass, she could still see her lying there.

It looked as if she was bathing. Not in water – but in the mist. Nona's mouth dropped open. Instinctively she hid behind the nearest tree. Castor flapped and cawed.

"Shh!" The last thing Nona wanted was to be spotted now. She wasn't ready to face this woman. Not yet. She needed some deep breaths first. In fact, she was struggling to find the courage to step out from behind the tree at all. She was certain now that she had dreamed this moment. That she'd already seen the woman at the centre of the stone circle. The déjà vu made her head spin. Worse, the memory of explosions, of falling bombs, rang in her ears, the scent of burning caught in her nose. Why was that night coming back to her now?

Nona's reflex to hide battled only against the voice in her head that urged her to run. To step out into the open, to show herself *on purpose* seemed reckless. But it felt like her legs had taken root. She couldn't get herself to move.

"Go on," said Castor, giving her hair a harder yank to encourage her to move. The shock of it turned Nona's frustration at her own failing courage into rage against Castor. She gritted her teeth. "Get off me, nasty bird!" She pushed him hard with one hand. Castor wobbled, opened out his wings and flew to the safety of a nearby branch.

"*Craaw.*"

"Shut up!"

"*Craaw!*"

Nona was having serious second thoughts, but at this rate Castor would give her away. Her heart pounded. She tried to slow her breathing and resist the urge to throw a punch. "I am not going down there," she hissed through a clenched jaw, "until you tell me who she is – and why she's done this. What does she want with my uncle, Castor? And what if … what if she puts a spell on me too?"

She was stalling, and by the look of things Castor knew it too. He clung hard to the tree branch and flapped his wings at her. "*Craaw.* You're too scared. Too scared."

"Shhh! I am *not* scared." How did he always manage to hit a sore spot? Nona took a swipe at him. But the gust Castor made with his wings made her eyes water and she missed. Castor took off.

"Castor. Wait. Come back!" It was too late. Castor had risen into the air and was circling back round towards the clearing, towards where the woman basked at the centre of the stone circle. Nona peered through the trees. There she was, plain as day. Castor cawed above the woman's head. The woman sat up. Her hair fell down past her shoulders in waves, adorned with wildflowers. At first she looked alarmed. Then she held out a long, slender hand, and Castor swooped down to perch on it.

Nona didn't want to look any more. She pressed herself as flat against the trunk of the tree as she could with her rucksack on and squeezed her eyes shut. Her heart thundered in her chest. She felt dizzy and sick with fear. "Castor, you traitor," she said under her breath. She hadn't been ready to face the woman. Then again, would she ever have been?

"Craaw!" came Castor's call. Nona opened her eyes in time to see him fly into the distance – back the way they'd come.

He'd given her away. And now, abandoned her. After she'd trusted him too.

Nona took a deep breath and held it in. Slowly she peered around the tree towards the stone circle. The mist. The woman.

The woman wasn't there.

"Nona," came a voice close to her ear. "You shouldn't be here." It was definitely the voice she'd heard coming from her uncle's painting room. Warm and silky-smooth, like honey.

Nona jerked her gaze away from the clearing. The woman – the spirit – was standing in front of her. Her flower-covered hair fell over a brown fur cape, made with the skin of some animal – a rabbit, perhaps, or hare – and fastened with a silver pin. She smiled slightly, although her grey-green eyes remained as cold as stone. "My name is Alesea," she said. "Come with me, Nona. Be quick. We mustn't linger here."

8

"WHO – *WHAT* ARE YOU?" SAID NONA. SHE COULDN'T
stop shaking. Nor could she prise her back away from
the tree. There was something else too: a feeling that
all her energy was draining away.

Alesea laughed. It was tuneful and relaxing, like
the pleasant burble of a stream. "This is nice," she
said once she'd finished. "I meet so many people,
but not always twice. As for what I am, I thought
Castor would have told you. I'm a spirit. A *guide* –
although probably not in the way you think." But
in an instant Alesea had paled. She glanced over
her shoulder, as if worried she might have been
overheard. It was the same face Nona might pull
if she'd been downstairs for a secret midnight
snack and had accidentally trodden on a creaky
floorboard.

Alesea's smile returned, though Nona could still see the fear in her eyes.

"What do you want with us?" demanded Nona. "Me and my uncle? Set him free."

Alesea didn't answer. "Such a remarkable girl," she said instead. The spirit reached out to touch Nona's scar. "Poor darling. So young, and you've been through a lot."

Nona jerked her head away. She'd had enough of being pecked, poked, pulled and prodded. And she hated the way Alesea was studying her. Looking at her scar. Alesea's face remained bright with humour, but her lips thinned slightly. She nodded and took her hand away. "And there's the strength I remember so well," she said, her eyes flashing.

Her comment passed Nona by. She was focused on just one thing. "Tell me what you've done to my Uncle Antoni," Nona said again.

"Very well." Alesea held out her hand, but this time as an offering. "Come with me and we'll talk. We shouldn't spend any longer here. It's dangerous." Alesea glanced over her shoulder again.

"Please," said Nona. Her teeth had started to chatter. Just speaking felt like a chore now. It was as if being close to this woman – Alesea – was draining her of energy. "Just tell me now," she struggled on.

"I don't want to go anywhere with you. I just want my uncle back. I saw you," she added, drawing laboured breaths, "in our studio. I know it was you. I—"

Nona stopped. She wanted to continue, to threaten Alesea with breaking the glass to prevent Uncle from working, but found that she couldn't. Her energy was all but gone. Only now did Alesea appear to notice. "You dear thing," she said, putting a hand to her own heart. "You're shivering. What do you need? Is it warmth? Or perhaps it's rest?" Then she drew back. "Did you not eat any of the food I left for you at the umbrafell? I put it there precisely to avoid this."

Nona shook her head. She saw no benefit in keeping that particular truth from Alesea. At any rate, her vision had started to grey around the edges, and she could no longer feel her legs below the knee. In a minute she might faint.

"Here." Alesea unpinned the fur cape from around her shoulders and reached out to wrap it around Nona. The fur repulsed her, reminding Nona of the lives that must have been taken to make it, and of the well-to-do people in the fancier end of the village who wore that sort of thing, who'd looked down their noses at her since the day she'd arrived from London. But she was too weak to resist. She let Alesea pull her forwards gently, away from the tree, in order to slip the cape around her shoulders.

"There you go." Alesea smiled, satisfied, and rubbed Nona's arms. "It suits you. Now to get you fed." Alesea wrapped an arm firmly around Nona and drew her in. Alesea felt soft. She smelled of amber and sweet flower pollen. Nestled against her, Nona felt peculiarly safe. The hug reminded her so much of her mother that she could hardly bear the ache in her heart.

Together they hurried towards the stone circle. The way Alesea kept checking over her shoulder made Nona nervous. She tried to ask again about her uncle but was too weak to insist on anything. Alesea rubbed Nona's shoulder and said, "There, there. All in good time."

The lights of a spirit path gathered around one of the stones. Nona had often seen this with the lights. They would lead her to a rock or a tree and then finish. But Alesea laid a hand against the stone, which was covered with blooms of white and yellow lichen. She smiled at Nona and although her lips didn't part, a whisper floated in the air.

All of a sudden, they moved forwards. But that was impossible. Ahead of them had only been the standing stone. No one could move *through* stone.

Nona's vision blurred. She buried her face against Alesea and squeezed her eyes shut to stop the world from spinning. A rushing – like a strong gale – overwhelmed her senses.

What was happening?

The next thing she became aware of was Alesea chatting amiably. "I assume you followed the spirit paths to find me. Clever! We spirits shed the smallest traces of our magic – light – behind us wherever we go. Which is why I must keep moving, you understand. Those of us like you and me who can see the lights don't all have your good intentions..." Nona could barely see through her greying vision by the time Alesea guided her down to perch on a large, flat rock, covered in moss. "Wait there," said Alesea, in her singsong voice. "This won't take long." She slipped away. And it was true: Nona could just make out the tiny lights Alesea left behind her that winked out like the fading embers of a fire.

Nona groaned and looked around. Her vision returned a little now she was resting. They were nowhere near the stone circle any more. Instead she found herself in a wood full of old, twisted trees with moss that hung from their branches like ancient lace. Frost, untouched by the early morning sun, made their trunks glitter silver.

A second ago they'd been in one place – and now they were in a different one altogether. None of this made sense. And she was still no closer to finding out what this "spirit" wanted from her uncle.

Thinking about too much at once made Nona's head spin with dizziness, and the dizziness made her feel sick. She could only wrap her arms around her head, rest it against her knees and wait for Alesea to come back.

This is not how she'd wanted her meeting with the spirit to go. At all. In her imaginings she'd been brave and in control when she confronted Alesea. Not small and frightened – and definitely not mysteriously drained by the spirit simply *being* there. This was just ... embarrassing.

"Here. Take this." Alesea's return gave Nona a start. She pressed something into Nona's palm. It was sticky but smelled divine. Honeycomb. Dripping with honey. "It will help you feel better," said Alesea. "I promise."

Although she didn't trust Alesea, Nona certainly couldn't feel any worse. Warily, she touched it to her lips. The sweet taste on her tongue banished her sickness instantly. She took a bigger bite. The honeycomb gave way satisfyingly against her teeth. She chewed. Now the greyness was receding, and she could see properly. After another bite she could sit upright again without being afraid of toppling over.

"That was amazing," said Nona, swallowing the last of the honeycomb. But even that didn't do justice to the taste. The war had ended several years ago, but plenty of food was still rationed and Nona hadn't eaten honey in years.

Alesea grinned and nodded. "I forget the effect I can have on people sometimes. Especially now that I keep so little company. But that honey should give you a little resistance." Nona felt a twinge of confusion. Although she refused to trust Alesea, she was grateful for feeling better. But now she needed to feed her curiosity.

"How did we get here?" asked Nona. Heat rose to her cheeks as she spoke and she still felt a bit shaky. She hoped Alesea couldn't see her flush.

"Through stone," Alesea replied simply. "Trees and rocks make excellent gateways to other places when you know how, and only a handful of us do. Far quicker than taking the human way, and a perfect way to stay hidden from—" But she said no more.

Nona's eyes widened. "Are we in the spirit world now?"

Alesea laughed. "No, silly! Just a different part on the moors. We took a shortcut." She swished her arm as she spoke, leaving a trail of lights that vanished in seconds.

"Those lights," Nona said, watching them fade. "Why do some disappear, and some stay?"

"They're traces of our magic, as I told you," came the reply. "But they fade quickly, unless we use the same route often – then they become permanent. Spirit paths. I can hide some using my power, but not all. That would take too long. Do you understand?"

Nona knitted her brow in thought. "You talk about magic," she said quietly. "But how can it possibly exist?" She was still struggling to comprehend.

"We harness light," said Alesea simply. "But we can't take it directly from the sun – only through reflection. Each of us has our own ways. I draw power from the moon, for example, while my spirit-sister Serafin, who you may meet soon, harvests it through water, and makes potions with the light energy stored inside plants."

Light? Nona knew all about that, working with glass. Uncle Antoni sometimes said that he wasn't a glass smith at all, but a manipulator of light. Still, it was too much for her to take in right now.

Now that Nona felt warmer, she unclasped the silver clip at her throat and handed the fur cape back to Alesea. Alesea fixed it in place on herself. She stroked the soft, brown, animal fur. With Nona's returning health came a renewed sense of urgency. Her uncle was still at the church under a spell. Alesea's spell.

Alesea, who had settled on a pillow of moss opposite, must have caught the expression on Nona's face. "You would no doubt like to know about your uncle," she said. "I'm sorry, Nona, but I had to put a *little* spell on him. It's for everyone's safety." Nona didn't understand. Uncle Antoni wouldn't hurt anyone.

"But—"

"The truth is," Alesea went on, twirling a small, white flower that she'd taken from her hair, "he's doing important work for me. But especially for you." She stopped twirling the flower and gave Nona a level stare.

Nona leaped to her feet. "What do you mean?" she said, shaking her head. "I don't want this." How could it be for her? She didn't know anything about it. She would never want Uncle Antoni to suffer this way for her sake. Ever.

"Let me explain," said Alesea, rising to her feet too. "Before it was destroyed in that ghastly war you had, the place you're staying in was special. Did Castor tell you why?"

"Because it … exists in the human world and the

spirit world at once?" said Nona, remembering. "He called it an umbrafell."

Alesea smiled. "That's right," she said. "Once it's complete again we can use its protective power in a spell that will both hide and shield you."

"Why? What do *I* need protecting from?"

For an instant Nona's mind drew back to the vision she'd seen last night – the silhouette of a towering man impressed on her closed eyelids. A chill settled over her like the frost that sparkled on the trees all around.

Alesea gave her a steady look. She took a step closer, then another, and whispered, "I think you already know."

9

NONA STARED AT ALESEA FOR A LONG TIME, UNABLE to reply. Could Alesea really know about her dreams and the visions her half-heart glass had shown her? How was that possible? Alesea narrowed her eyes.

"You see things, don't you?" she said. "I can tell. You've seen *him*."

Nona bit her lip. "I ... I have dreamed of someone," she admitted. Her fingers tightened around the glass fragment in her pocket, bundled in hankies. "I can't see his face," she went on, "but he has animal horns, and a cape, and something glowing in his chest and—" Nona broke off. The spirit had paled and fear had flooded her eyes.

"I see lots of things other people don't, actually," Nona said. She saw no harm in telling Alesea – a magical being. Perhaps, as a spirit, Alesea might even be able to explain some of it. "Like the lights from the spirit paths. I didn't know that's what they were until Castor told me. And people. I saw you." Nona paused. "But the dreams… They mostly come when I sleep next to this. I can see things when I hold it too." Nona pulled the glass fragment from her pocket, unwrapped one pink edge and held it out to Alesea to take. "Want to look?"

Alesea took a step back. "No!"

Startled, Nona wrapped the glass up and slipped it back into her skirt pocket. Silence lingered between them. "Castor called it enchanted," Nona said finally, with caution. "Is that why I can see things other people can't?"

Alesea raised an eyebrow. "Yes, and no. Your abilities exist without it – but your glass enhances them. It stores light magic." Then her face softened. "I'm sorry I was abrupt just now, darling. You surprised me with it, that's all. Spirits can't touch glass. We can look through it to the human world, and occasionally we can be glimpsed from the other side … but to touch it hurts us and drains our power. Glass is human alchemy. Years ago you sealed your homes with it to keep us on one side and yourselves on the other, and you made vessels to trap the power of any of us who came near. And just like that, the spirit and human worlds were pushed apart, separated. You were frightened, I expect," said Alesea, raising an eyebrow, "and you had your own deities by then."

"I don't understand," said Nona. "You can look through glass, but not touch it?"

"Glass stores power. Light magic. If a spirit touches it their magic is drawn inside."

A thought struck Nona. "Is that why you need my uncle to do the windows of the umbrafell? Because you can't touch the glass?"

Alesea nodded.

"But then why would you want glass in the church, if it hurts you? And what were you doing in Uncle's studio?"

"Questions, questions!" laughed Alesea. "A little glass here and there is no problem for me when I know where to expect it." She waved her hand. "I was cautious not to touch any when I came to visit, but the urgency outweighed the danger. I had no choice but to seek out Antoni Pilecki, you see, whom you call your uncle."

Nona didn't like the way Alesea smiled when she said the word "uncle". Just because they weren't related, it didn't make them any less close. She clenched her jaw. Together they were a family. Even though sometimes – only sometimes – she felt guilty for moving on.

It crossed Nona's mind that she could use the glass to threaten Alesea. Then Alesea would have to release her uncle. But it actually felt more like Alesea was trying to help her now. Not that she believed she could trust this woman, exactly, and she was patronising, but what more could Alesea tell Nona? About her dreams? Her ability to see the spirit paths?

"As for why this is necessary," the spirit went on, "an umbrafell that brings together both human and spirit magic is destined to be a powerfully protected place. And it may be our only hope of surviving him."

The chill ran through Nona's blood again. "So this … *shadow* I keep seeing," she said. "What does he want?"

Alesea suddenly bent forwards and clasped Nona's hands in hers. They felt soft and cool. Their touch made Nona's fingers a little numb. "He's a sorcerer called the Soldier," she said. "He was human once – and a real soldier. But something … happened." Alesea's face remained a mask to her true feelings, but her eyes flashed. "Now he's part-spirit too, which makes him dangerous. His human side allows him to touch glass. So he's built himself a monstrous glass heart." Alesea said this part with dread in her voice and clasped Nona's hands tighter. Her eyes had grown dark. "It's to trap and store ever more power – *spirit* magic, taken from us. It's prolonged his life for many years. There's every chance he may be immortal now. But what he really wants..." She paused, gathering her calm again. "What he really wants is to become powerful enough to raise the dead."

"Why?" Nona gasped, although a thought stirred instantly in her mind. What she wouldn't give to be able to bring back her mother and brother. Alesea didn't answer, but pulled away one hand to touch the silver pin at her throat and looked over her shoulder again. Nona wished she wouldn't keep doing that. It unnerved her.

Her mind was racing. Could this really be true? And even if it was, what did any of it have to do with *her*?

As if sensing her doubt, Alesea withdrew and straightened. A smile crossed her lips – not amused, but an attempt to be friendly, perhaps. Or to trick her? To make Nona trust her when she shouldn't?

"Believe me or don't, you are in danger," said Alesea, "And this is still necessary. As for why," she continued, "years ago, after the first war in which he fought – the Great War, you call it – the Soldier had a son he lost to illness. The Soldier wishes to bring him back at all costs. Even if it means stealing spirit magic and ... sacrificing another."

The words hit Nona like a cold stab to the gut. She knew what it felt like to lose loved ones. And if there was any way to bring them back, she would do it. She could almost feel sorry for this "Soldier" if it wasn't for that last bit. "Sacrificing another?" Nona mumbled into her chest. "What do you mean?" Her skin had started to prickle. She thought she could guess.

"He's tried many things," said Alesea quietly. "Animating lifeless objects, for example... He's come close. Very close. But ten days ago he learned of a way that could bring back his son. Life must be exchanged for life, Nona," she said, her eyes sparkling. "And the Soldier wants to sacrifice *yours* for his son's."

Nona felt stunned. Her lungs tightened as though they had rope tied around them. "W-why me?" she managed to say. Her throat felt hoarse and scratchy. What was so special about her? She'd never met this Soldier in her life. She'd only just heard of him.

"Because you have a touch of spirit magic, Nona, just like him. Think of the things you can see that others can't. But first, he needs your glass," she turned her gaze to Nona's pocket, where the half-heart nestled, "to complete the heart he's made for himself and strengthen his power. Then he needs your life."

"But—" Horror rippled through Nona. Her whole body had turned ice cold. Alesea had to have made a mistake, surely. How did this Soldier even know about her?

From somewhere close by, a twig snapped. Followed by a creaking noise. Alesea grabbed Nona's shoulder. "Quickly," she hissed. "Run!"

Before Nona knew it, they were running: dodging around rocks and roots. Alesea was fast – but Nona was agile and could think on her feet. She darted around trees, over rocks and under branches, all while keeping pace with Alesea. Her heart pounded. What were they running from? Nona had no idea, but Alesea's fright was infectious.

The air rushing past her ears, it was impossible to hear anything else – to tell if they'd left whatever it was behind or if they were still being pursued. "Wait," gasped Nona. "What are you so scared of? Is the Soldier coming?"

Alesea didn't reply.

Their best bet was to hide, Nona thought: to gather themselves. At this rate they'd have every chance of running straight into the thing they were trying to run *from*. Alesea didn't seem to be thinking clearly. That's when Nona spotted a small but steep slope that looked like it had a slight overhang.

That ought to at least provide some cover.

"Over here!" Nona darted towards it and slid down using her hands for balance. The earth crumbled underfoot as she did so, exposing tangles of young roots like grasping, bony fingers.

Alesea grabbed Nona's arm and yanked her away before seeming to realize they were harmless. She took a deep breath and let Nona go. They waited, silent, listening. But no more sounds came. The peace of the ancient wood enclosed them.

Adrenalin thrummed through Nona's body. She rubbed her arm where Alesea had grabbed her. Alesea noticed and said, "I'm sorry if I hurt you, darling. I thought…"

"You thought what?" asked Nona, her voice low. "What are we running from? It's the same thing you're always looking over your shoulder for, isn't it? Tell me."

Alesea paused. Then she hissed, "Rattlesticks. The Soldier's minions. His … *experiments*." Alesea clammed up and took a step away.

"Please, explain," said Nona, sensing that Alesea was preparing to leave her. "What are they – and why does the Soldier want to sacrifice me? I don't understand!" Panic swelled inside her chest, making it difficult to breathe.

"Soon, Nona, but not now," Alesea said, her voice still low but firm. "We've spent too long together already. As soon as your uncle has completed the windows of the umbrafell I will free him, I promise. Until then, you and I must keep our distance as much as we can."

Alesea was already backing away. "Wait!" said Nona. "I don't know where I am or how to get back. Are we safe now? How do I even know if this Soldier is the same figure I've dreamed, and if it isn't, how will I know what to stay away from?"

Another strange creaking sound came from the woods.

Alesea flinched and said in a hurry, "You'll be safer without me here. But if you need to see for yourself, to be certain it's the Soldier you've seen..." Alesea stroked the soft, brown fur of her cape. She pinched some of the hairs between her fingers and plucked them out. "Take these hairs to Castor, tonight," she said. "He'll show you what to do. You'll see for yourself why I run. And why you must too. Why we all have to stay hidden – from him, and from those ... *things* he sends after us. The rattlesticks. But be careful, Nona. Even a small spell such as this has its risks."

Nona took the hairs. Three of them, deep brown at one end, lightening to hazel, with white tips.

Definitely real fur, from some sort of wild animal. She fished out a spare hankie from her pocket and folded them away for safekeeping.

When she looked up again, Alesea was gone. The only sign of life other than the trees themselves was a hare darting away through the mossy rocks.

Nona had no doubt that the hare was Alesea. That it had been her, in animal form, who had watched them intently from the middle of the road when Nona and her uncle first arrived at the church. But now she was alone, with no idea how she would find the church, or Uncle Antoni, again. And what she'd learned about the Soldier – about his intention to sacrifice her – clouded her mind with terror, blotting out all else.

IO

NONA SET OFF OUT OF THE WOODS, CHECKING behind her every few steps to make sure she wasn't being followed. Alesea's reaction to those noises had left her with a creeping dread.

Those things *that he sends after us*, she had said. Nona shuddered. Rattlesticks, Alesea had called them. Were they related to the Soldier's attempt to raise the dead? Hadn't Alesea said something about the Soldier animating lifeless objects?

The wind whipped across the plains as Nona walked, and needled her through the holes in her jumper. Grey clouds rolled over the sky. Swathes of mist appeared all around and left just as quickly, obscuring her way. It was hard to know which direction she was going.

She couldn't even see any of the lights from the

spirit paths, which would at least have given her something to follow.

Would the glass be able to help her? Nona pulled the fragment from her pocket and unwrapped it. But when she held it to the light she saw nothing. She turned it this way, and that, moved round in a circle. Still nothing.

Nona rubbed the surface with her thumb. It left a smear of moisture which slowly faded. The Soldier needed it to complete his power, Alesea had said. And he wanted to sacrifice her – Nona's – life for his son's. But why her, when she'd known nothing of him until recently? And how was it that she could see the spirits and their paths in the first place? She was only human after all. Between Alesea and Castor, they'd told her that her glass half-heart was enchanted, but it only *enhanced* her abilities. What did that mean?

She didn't have time to puzzle over it now. She had to get back to her uncle.

Finally, Nona found herself in a valley between two great rolling hills. One side was good and tall: she ought to be able to see more clearly from up there. It was a hard trudge to the top, and Nona's legs already ached. She passed a pony, chewing shrub, that watched as she went by. Nona thought of the honeycomb she'd eaten earlier. It was the only food she'd had all day. Her stomach growled.

At the highest point, Nona glanced around. Nothing but endless moorland. Grass and sky. Patches of mist. She didn't recognize any of it. And she couldn't see the church at all. She wished she had Castor to guide her – even if his manner of orienteering was likely to cause her injury. She felt bad for getting so angry with him now when all he'd done was lead her to Alesea like she'd asked – although she was still annoyed that he'd given her away to Alesea and then just left her there.

"Castor," she shouted in desperation. "Where are you?" Her voice blanched in the strength of the wind, and Castor didn't come.

Nona's skin prickled. That feeling she was being watched again. She thought of the Soldier – of what he apparently intended to do with her. She walked in a slow circle and scanned the horizon. She couldn't even see the wood now. The sky darkened. A little icy sleet began to fall.

Panic rose in her chest. Everything began to blur. Nona took a few deep breaths, but the fear buzzed inside her like swarming bees. What if she couldn't find her way back to her uncle, ever? Pain – from the cold sleet and from the clamour in her brain – sliced at her temple and she lowered her head and cradled her skull in her hands. She had to calm down. She groaned. The soothing vibration of her own voice travelling through her body actually made her head hurt less. Again, she tried to control her panic. *Think*, Nona urged herself. *What would Uncle Antoni do?*

Draw, he would tell her. Drawing would bring back her focus.

She took shelter beside an angled rock. There she fumbled with her rucksack and brought out the sketchbook and pencil, sat cross-legged and began to draw with a shaking hand, shielding the paper from wind and sleet with her own hunched body. At first her lines were rushed and based on nothing beyond her own terror: the rapid, wavy lines of hills, stretching back, and back, and back. Until slowly, surely, she could pick out some of the things in front of her. A tree. A tor. Cloud patterns.

This is what Uncle Antoni had got her doing – from the first day she'd come to live with him and he'd discovered she liked to trace patterns and pictures on things with her fingers. If she was upset, or panicked, or tried to talk about the dead, he'd plonk her in front of a flower instead, or a pretty vase, or a picture of a person, and say, "Draw what's in front of you. Focus on nothing else. Not what's in your head, not the past, but what's in front of your eyes. The past's gone, Jenny Wren. Best leave it there."

Nona couldn't help feeling what he meant was that she ought to forget her past. Push it away. And what if she didn't want to? She missed her mother and brother desperately. Would they be sad if they could know she'd forgotten them? And for all his artistry, all his focus, Uncle still had his nightmares.

Everything he drew was beautiful, though. Whether he used a pencil or a paintbrush, it was as though he wielded a magic wand. Every flick and flourish brought the most wondrous things into being. It wasn't the same for Nona. She practised and worked, and worked and practised, and yet the darkness inside her head always seeped onto the page. Her drawings came out ... damaged. Like ugly stains.

She hoped to learn Uncle's secret one day.

She realized the technique had begun to work. She could feel her panic lifting like mist and her mind clearing. The landscape in front of her made more sense. She could see small details beyond her hill now, like tracks and walls. What had to be the remains of an Iron Age fort. And then, with a surge of relief, she spotted the stone circle where she'd first met Alesea.

From there, the roads, the ruined church and the few empty houses around it were easy to spot: a dark cluster of stone. It was still far away. Alesea had clearly forgotten that Nona was no spirit, and couldn't take a shortcut. Nona clenched her jaw. She'd be having words with Castor when she finally got back – for leaving her.

As Nona picked up her sketchbook to tuck it away in her bag, something caught her eye. A convergence of darkness at the centre of the page, on the horizon she'd drawn. She ran her finger over it, slightly smudging the heavy lead. It almost looked like the shape of a person inside all that darkness. In the midst of her anxiety she hadn't realized. Nona shuddered, noting how similar it was to last night's dream of the Soldier. What more proof did she need that the things in her head always seeped onto the page?

With the way ahead and several landmarks committed to memory, Nona set off down the hill again – towards the place where her uncle toiled. Where, when it was finally finished, Nona would apparently be protected – from a man with a glass heart who wanted to sacrifice her. A man who couldn't die.

❧❧❧❧

By the time Nona made it back to the church, the early February dusk was drawing in. She'd spent all day on the moors. Her stomach cramped with hunger.

But Nona couldn't wait to see her uncle. Would he be free from Alesea's spell again for the evening?

Her legs felt as if they might give way at any second, but she charged through the church door. "Uncle!" she called out. Her stomach growled, but she barely noticed. Uncle Antoni was exactly where she'd left him: hunched over his sketches. He didn't turn to greet her.

Nona covered her face with her hands. Fatigue and sadness crashed over her.

"Calm down," said a voice by her ear – one she recognized. "The sun hasn't gone properly yet. When it does, he'll be free, you mark my words."

Castor – in his imp form. He looked a particularly steely silver this evening. "You!" Nona snatched at his leg. Castor jumped away from her grasping hand just in time. "You told her where I was." Nona swiped for him again. Again, Castor dodged. "And you left me there with her. I've been walking in circles all day."

"I had to," he shot back, "or you'd never have come out from that tree. You'd still be hiding." Castor pulsed a deep orange, which made him look for a minute like glowing coals. Nona gritted her teeth. Her ears and cheeks burned red-hot.

"You pecked me," she growled, staring him in the eye. "And pulled my hair. It hurt."

"It can't have," he grumbled, but his orange glow paled to yellow as if he'd been extinguished. "You must have a very soft sort of a head."

"My head's no different than any other person's." Nona gritted her teeth and stood poised to lunge again. "Don't try to make excuses."

But Castor was turning a sickly light green all over. His tummy, Nona noticed, was not scaly but soft and pale and a little spotted, like a newt's. He crouched low to the floor. "All right," he said after a pause. "I'm sorry. I didn't mean to hurt you or I wouldn't have." He lowered his head so that he was practically talking to the floor. "When I'm a crow it's harder to show what I mean without words. The beak's pretty useful…"

"It's pretty sharp, is what it is," said Nona. "And then you just flew off and I got lost getting back."

"Will you leave now?" asked Castor. He shot her a quick glance but returned his gaze to the floor. His face looked forlorn. "I'll be all right if you do, you know. I've been alone for a long time. I'm … used to not having friends."

Nona softened. She walked closer and sat on a pew near him. Was that what he'd wanted all along? He made her think of a kid at times. Just one who'd been on their own for a long time. Clearly he'd been lonely. She knew what that felt like.

They sat in silence for a few moments, as the dusk light flooding in through the church windows darkened beneath passing clouds. Nona sighed. "I don't think I could leave, even if I wanted to," she said, glancing at Uncle Antoni. Out of the corner of her eye, she noticed deep blue ripple across Castor's scales. "But if we're going to be friends," she added, glancing over at him, "I don't want any more pecking or hair pulling. And don't leave me in the middle of nowhere again. All right?"

Castor flashed and pulsed with colour.

"You've got to remember that I'm not a crow," Nona added.

"I promise not to pull your hair again. And I definitely won't peck," he said. "Ever, ever again. If I feel like doing it, I'll just go and eat a beetle instead."

"Ummm. That's good," agreed Nona uncertainly. "And to be fair, it was Alesea who really left me in the middle of nowhere." They smiled at each other. "Actually," Nona added, "there's something I have to do. And I don't know how. Alesea said you might be able to help…"

Castor's ears pricked. He didn't look at her, but a little shiver of purple ran across his scales. Nona fished her handkerchief out of her pocket and carefully unwrapped it to reveal the three hairs Alesea had pulled from her cape.

"Ooh," said Castor. "A spell! What spell?"

Nona jumped so high she almost dropped the whole lot, hankie and all. He'd climbed onto the pew next to Nona without her noticing and pressed his face close to the hairs. Luckily she held onto them. "So you can help with that kind of thing?" she asked, once she'd recovered from the shock. "Alesea said they're to show me the Soldier."

Castor shrank back from her like a cat into the shadows, until all she could see were his huge, round eyes, staring at her. They were a dark, midnight blue.

A screech of chair legs against tiles and a yell from over near the altar made Nona jump to her feet. She spun around. Uncle Antoni had pushed out his chair and was standing, staring all around, as if he'd just woken from a nightmare.

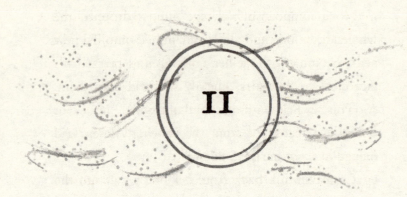

11

"What is this? Nona? What—" Uncle Antoni seemed confused – and scared. Nona bundled the hairs inside her handkerchief, stuffed it in her pocket and rushed to his side.

"It's all right, Uncle." She clutched him round the shoulders. "We're in Dartmoor, remember? We've come to fix the windows…" Nona didn't want to remind him of everything at once for fear of overwhelming him. Just the basics would do for now.

"What have I been doing all day? Why can't I remember?"

"You've been working, Uncle." They looked at his cartoons, most now complete, the lead he'd stretched and even some glass pieces he'd already cut. Though the windows were far from ready and, Nona thought with a shiver, she wouldn't be safe until they were.

"Oh, Jenny Wren." His shoulders relaxed a little and he drew Nona into a hug. "I'm exhausted. Let's have a brew on the Primus, eh?" Nona smiled. She scanned the room for Castor as she settled Uncle Antoni down on a pew, but he'd hidden himself again.

This time Nona used supplies from the altar. She had already eaten the honey in the woods, and it had helped her, not harmed. She boiled some of the fresh eggs to have with their bread and scrape, with a bowl of wild berries and more honey for after.

The food rejuvenated Uncle Antoni at first, but soon he could barely keep his eyes open after his day of non-stop work. Nona knew from before that he would soon fall into a deep, still sleep.

Once they were both fed and watered, Nona helped her uncle up the stairs. "I'm sorry about all this, Jenny Wren," he said, already closing his eyes as Nona tucked him into his bed. "Tomorrow I'll be more with it. I just need some sleep and then I'll be fine."

Nona stroked his hand and said nothing as shadows shifted across his face. In moments he began to snore.

A cool palm rested against Nona's back, and its small, bulbous fingers gave her a gentle pat. It didn't surprise her or make her jump. She'd guessed Castor would make his appearance as soon as her uncle was asleep. The careful gentleness of his touch made her smile. He was clearly making an effort. "Hello, Castor," she said.

Now for the spell.

Nona pulled the hankie out of her pocket and opened it out carefully to check that the hairs were still inside. "So ... you haven't forgotten about that, then." Castor's voice sounded more serious than Nona had ever heard it. She remembered how frightened he'd looked when she'd told him what they were for. As soon as she'd mentioned the Soldier.

"No. I haven't forgotten," Nona said. "Is it... I mean, is he really that bad?" She turned to Castor and looked him full in the face. Castor, wide-eyed and solemn, held her gaze. He nodded.

"The Soldier is so bad that even summoning his image, like we're about to, is dangerous. If he sensed us watching him..." The imp shuddered, bristling white all over. "Are you sure you want to do it?"

Nona thought about it. This Soldier sounded like he was best left well alone. But he was the one coming for *her*, and ignoring that fact wouldn't change anything. She had to know for certain if it was the same shadowy figure she'd seen in her dreams. To see for herself. It wouldn't feel real otherwise.

With gritted teeth, Nona met Castor's gaze. 'Let's get it over with,' she said.

Nona fetched a candle and some matches on Castor's instruction and met him back on the second floor. But Castor wasn't there.

"Castor?" she called.

"Up here!" came his voice. It seemed to come from an open wooden hatch in the roof with a small set of steps leading up to it. She hadn't noticed it before. Perhaps it was where Castor could come and go from, as a crow.

Castor's face appeared on the other side of the hatch which led to the roof. "Don't worry. I'll catch you if you fall."

"You?" She laughed in disbelief. "You'd never be able to hold my weight."

"Well, you can't have *everything*. Fine, fine. You don't have to come all the way out. Just a bit of you will do." Nona rolled her eyes and climbed the steps to the hatch. Pushing herself through was actually a lot easier than she'd expected, and she surprised herself by squeezing all the way out of the hatch to join Castor on the very top of the roof. At that height she could see the nearby rooftops of deserted cottages, and beyond those the moorland touching the horizon, the sky, the moon. She breathed in the clean, icy air to steady herself.

"Now light the candle," said Castor. Nona struck a match, kept it low and shielded it from the wind that was blowing her hair around in gusts. Once she'd melted enough of the bottom of the candle and jammed it against the stone so that the melted wax was stuck in place, she lit the wick. The flame began as a small orb, then stretched slowly upwards like a creature coming out of hiding.

"Good," said Castor. "I'll make sure it doesn't go out. You get the hairs." He cupped his small hands around the flame, while Nona unwrapped her handkerchief. She pinched the hairs tight between her fingers to stop them from blowing away.

"Now what?" she asked.

"Now you eat the hairs while chanting: 'Yum, yum, a hairy tum!'"

Nona stared at Castor and then at the hairs in disgust. "What?"

The imp's laughter echoed out into the night sky in shrieks and whoops, as wild as the wind. "Sorry," he said once he'd composed himself. "I couldn't help it. I joke when I'm scared."

"You have a strange sense of humour," grumbled Nona.

Castor shifted closer to the candle in a squat, his hands still cupped around the flame. That forked tail of his swished from side to side, like a cat's. "Burn the hairs in the flame," said Castor, serious now. "And then we'll say: 'Show us the one who cheated death. Show us the Soldier,' together. All right?"

Nona nodded and brought the hairs to the flame. In a split-second they blackened, crinkled and curled, a stream of dark smoke rising from the candle. Nona breathed some of it in. The acrid stink made her choke before the smoke caught on the wind and streamed away from her into the sky.

"Show us the one who cheated death," said Castor and Nona together. "Show us the Soldier."

Castor studied the sky. Nona followed his gaze, but there was nothing there. Nothing except clouds rolling fast across the sky with the wind.

For a moment the clouds covered the moon. The shadow passed across their faces. When it thinned and parted and the moonlight slipped through again, Castor pointed urgently to the horizon. "Look!" he hissed.

Just above the line of the horizon, darker clouds gathered above the large shape of a man, black in silhouette. The clouds didn't roll away as the others did but seemed to gather over the figure – almost as if they were a part of him, or being channelled *into* him. Nona squinted to try to see better. The figure's body was broad and long, as if he wore a fur cape like Alesea's, but one that trailed all the way to the floor. He looked human, except for his head. The head was that of some sort of horned animal, like a stag. Nona moaned with the realization: it really was the same as her dreams. As her drawing, earlier. And there, if she squinted still harder, was the red glow emanating from his chest – like a distant fire. When he'd just been a vision in her mind's eye – and when she only had Alesea's word for it – she could still just about pretend he wasn't real. That this wasn't happening. Not any more.

"Haven't you seen enough?" said Castor in the same urgent hiss before. "Let's snuff out the candle quick, before he starts to suspect that he's being spied on."

"Even if he suspects, he wouldn't actually be able to *see* us. Would he?" Nona said.

"If we can see him, he could see us," said Castor.

"What?" Nona stared again at the Soldier. Impossibly tall with the head of a beast, and all those dark clouds drawing around him like a shroud. The sight of him turned her stomach to lead.

"That's him all right," said Castor, filling the silence. "The Soldier. Most likely can't ever die, now he has that accursed glass heart. Can't be stopped, no matter what Alesea and Serafin reckon. It's only a matter of time before—" Castor looked at Nona with his lips sucked in, as though he'd said too much. "Sorry."

Nona had other problems, though. She was finding it hard to breathe. The stench from the burned hairs clung in her throat and her fear squeezed her lungs. She turned back to the Soldier. She didn't want to look. She wanted him to disappear and never come back. But something in her brain nagged at her until she looked. It was as if his form was magnetic, as if his presence drew everything towards it.

She dug her hand into her pocket to seek out the comfort of the half-heart and gripped it tight.

As she watched, the figure on the horizon changed. It was almost imperceptible, but Nona felt it in her body as much as she saw it. The Soldier had been moving forwards – ever forwards. And now he stopped. He turned his horned, skull head towards them…

Nona's whole body went cold.

"The candle!" shrieked Castor in a harsh whisper. Nona snuffed the flame in a hurry with her bare fingers. It hissed and stung her fingertips. The candle went out.

The vision of the Soldier remained.

※※※※※

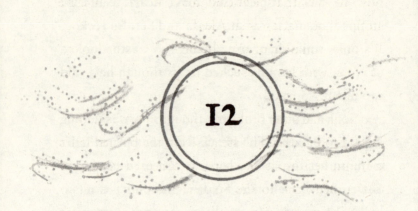

12

NONA DREW BACK IN HORROR. "WHY IS HE STILL there?" she asked Castor. "You said he'd disappear when the candle went out."

Castor looked from Nona to the horizon and back again. "He isn't. He did disappear."

"No. I can still see him." Nona flattened herself against the roof.

Castor hopped up and down, squinting. "What? Where?"

"There!" Nona pointed. "He never left."

Castor stopped jumping and stared at her, his eyes wide and horrified. "You didn't breathe in any of the smoke, did you?" he asked.

"Yes, I think so. Why?" Nona could still smell the burned hair – as well as taste it in the back of her throat.

"You what? I specifically told you not to breathe in the smoke," Castor shrieked.

"No, you didn't," she groaned.

"Didn't I?"

"No."

"Ugh." Castor slumped against the stone. "Well, I meant to. Come on." He waved his hands at her in a frantic gesture. "The sooner we get off this roof the better. Before he notices you and sends—"

A noise from downstairs stopped him mid-sentence. It sounded like the kind of sound the bough of a tree might make as it rubbed against itself – a long, drawn out creak. Like the sound Nona had heard in the woods with Alesea. They both held their breath and listened.

There it was again. Another drawn out creak. And then the clack-clacking of something hard against stone. Footsteps of some sort. This time it came from inside.

"It's too late," whispered Castor. "If we hide up here, it might go away. Eventually."

"What might?" Nona's heart was pounding against the rooftiles.

"The rattlestick." Castor's voice was filled with dread. "The Soldier probably sent it to investigate. You used magic and he can see you now, remember?

He probably wants to find out who you are. He knows most things about the one he's after except what you look like. He can't find out it's you he needs…"

"Castor. What exactly is a rattlestick?" breathed Nona. Both of them were speaking as quietly as they possibly could and a cold sweat had started to prickle Nona's forehead.

"Look down there," said Castor, "and you'll see." Nona manoeuvred along the roof to the hatch and peered through. From there she had a clear line of sight all the way past the upper balconies to the ground floor. Something thin and white was shuffling around there. Nona gripped the edges of the hatch harder than ever. It looked like a skeleton. A human one. And the way it moved – creeping stealthily while looking first left, then right – it was clearly searching for something. For them.

And Uncle Antoni was on the upper floor, sleeping.

"The Soldier raises them from the ground," said Castor close to her ear. "They're made of sticks and stones. Old roots. Petrified wood. That kind of thing. Any old bit of tat. They aren't alive as such … they're controlled by him. They only come out at night or in shadowy places. Some are scouts, like this one. His informants. Others are magic stealers. He sends those after the spirits to drain their power.

Both types are pretty easy to knock over and break, but if they touch you, you'll turn into one. And that'll be the end of you."

"But doesn't the Soldier need me as a..." She couldn't bring herself to say the word: sacrifice. "So they wouldn't turn me into one of them. Would they?" More shuffling came from inside the umbrafell, no doubt as the rattlestick went about searching.

"He wouldn't bat an eyelid if his rattlesticks got you," Castor whispered. "If they did, all the better! No need to bother with a sacrifice then. Your life force would flow to him through his creature and get bottled up in that weird heart. Then all he'd need is that glass of yours to make him strong enough to use it. Anyway. He believes in a prophesied time, so he probably doesn't think it could happen. We'll just stay here on the roof, to be safe," whispered Castor, even more quietly. "Until it gives up and goes away."

Nona had no desire to confront that thing. But what about Uncle?

"Uncle Antoni's asleep down there," hissed Nona. "He's in danger." She couldn't just stay here hiding behind the curve of the roof. As quietly as she could, Nona edged her way down through the hatch and onto the upper floor. Castor hung upside down through the hatch to glare at her.

"Wait," he said. "Didn't you hear what I said? All it has to do is touch you and you'll become one of them."

"Exactly. I can't leave Uncle Antoni to get turned into one of those creatures," she replied. "You said they're easy to stop. What if I dropped something on it?" Their conversation was little more than mouthed now.

"Best get it first time if you're going to do that," said Castor, lowering himself through the gap to perch on her shoulder. Nona looked around and spotted the large pestle and mortar she'd used to threaten Castor with only yesterday. It was still on the floor where she'd put it. She took out the long pestle and carried the mortar over to the balcony with both hands, waiting for the rattlestick to come into view. She could hear it clunking around. Hear its body creaking and clicking. Uncanny, how human it looked, Nona thought. How skeletal. It made the hairs on her neck stand on end.

The rattlestick moved slowly, deliberately. Nona waited. It threaded through the pews. Up and down each of the rows. Nona's palms started to sweat. Finally it stopped right below her. That was the moment she'd been waiting for.

Nona let the mortar go.

Perhaps the creature felt the air move or sensed her standing above it at the last second. Because it looked up and side-stepped in one swift move. The mortar landed with a crash that resounded around the walls – right by the rattlestick's foot. And now it had seen them.

The creature stared at Nona with dark, hollow eyes, before skittering out of sight, fast. It had to be heading for the stairs.

"I thought I told you to get it the first time," shrieked Castor. There was no point being quiet now – the rattlestick had seen them and it was coming.

"It's not my fault," said Nona, staring around wildly for something else to throw. "It moved!"

Castor pressed his hands against the floor and muttered some words. When he took his palm away, a pile of small rocks had appeared. "A little trick I learned," he said with a humourless grin. "Comes in handy sometimes, hanging around with spirits."

There was no time to marvel at Castor's trick. Nona gathered up some of the rocks and so did Castor. They ran to the stairs. If they could catch the creature on the staircase, it would have less space to move and so less chance of dodging them.

They heard it before they saw it. That ominous clacking of stone against stone. Then it rounded the curve in the stairwell. Nona didn't think. Just started hurling stones. So did Castor. The first few missed: one fell at its feet, while several of Castor's smaller stones whistled past its head. Nona was out of rocks. She grabbed the heavy pestle she'd taken out of the mortar and hurled it.

The pestle caught the skeletal creature full in the chest. It broke into fragments in a split second, which spilled all over the steps and lay there: nothing but blanched twigs, quartz and stone, pieces of old root. Just as Castor had described.

Nona sank to the floor. It took a while to steady her nerves. Once she had, she glanced behind her to check on Uncle Antoni. He still slumbered peacefully in his bed – dead to the world.

If the rattlestick had found him, Uncle Antoni wouldn't have stood a chance.

I3

NONA CLAMBERED OVER THE SCATTERED PIECES OF
the rattlestick, all the way down the stairs to the lower
floor, where she sat among her uncle's designs and
hugged her knees. It was hard to take in everything
she'd seen and learned. That this Soldier could see
her now. And he had creatures at his command: these
strange and terrifying rattlesticks.

Would it only be a matter of time before he came
after her again? Maybe more were coming right now.

In spite of her fear, Nona couldn't help noticing
the beauty of Uncle Antoni's drawing. It didn't
matter that the "cartoons", as they were called, were
technical plans to help with the eventual cutting of
the glass. Uncle Antoni drew with flair.

Gloomy thoughts rumbled around Nona's
mind like storm clouds. Until Castor appeared and

immediately began to pace. "You'll just have to stay hidden as much as possible," he said. "Until you get your second skin. It's lucky that he doesn't have a clue what the one he's out to get actually looks like, or that would've been it. That means you, by the way. As far as he knows you could've been any old kid mucking about with things they don't understand, who did real magic by accident. It does happen. Once is suspicious, yes. But twice would be a dead giveaway. Just keep hoping he doesn't spot you again and send any more rattlesticks. Or that he doesn't sense that thing." Castor gestured at Nona's pocket: he must mean the half-heart glass. "Stay out of sight as much as you can. Yes." He seemed to be talking to himself now. "That's the only way."

The Soldier didn't know what she looked like. That was something, at least. Knowing that made her stomach twist a little less. But she'd raised his suspicion, enough to send a rattlestick after them. Had she put the whole plan for the umbrafell at risk? And there was more she didn't understand. How did Alesea know she was the one the Soldier was after when *he* didn't? Could Alesea be wrong?

"What's a second skin?" Nona asked, after Castor had finished ranting.

"You know." Castor sounded irritated. "The way

Alesea turns into a hare and the Soldier is what he is, and I'm—" He froze. "We could get you a coat. A nice furry coat for the time being, with ears on. He'll think you're a deer."

A smile had broken out across Nona's face before she could stop it. "Be serious," she said. Dark thoughts swooped on her again and she sighed deeply. The tree growing through the church floor filtered moonlight through its branches. It looked eerie and beautiful all at once. Amazing to think that this little tree had sewn the worlds together, creating this powerful place. She tried to concentrate on the beauty of it instead of the inner voice that nagged at her to peer out of the window. To check on the Soldier's progress.

"Dear little face," said Castor, reaching out all of a sudden to squish Nona's cheeks. "We'll stick some leaves over it. You'll be fine."

How did Castor manage to be so funny and annoying at the same time? Nona half-laughed. There was no way she was going to let Castor stick leaves on her face. Or anything else. Although she was beginning to trust him, and even to like him, there were limits. "Thanks," she said. "But I'll be all right without the leaves."

"Hmm. If you say so. As long as you stay hidden for the rest of the night, we shouldn't have any more rattlestick trouble. That one was just a scout. Nothing serious. The Soldier would only expect to hear back from it if there was a problem, and he won't hear back from it, because we smashed it. So he won't bother sending more. I think… And hope."

"Let me see if I understand," said Nona. "He can see me now, but until now he hasn't seen my face, so he can't know for sure I'm the one he's looking for. Is that it?"

"Exactly! I think. And hope," said Castor. "And that's the way we need to keep it. The not knowing part. All right? Anyway, good night, Nona. Sleep well!"

Castor shrugged and scrunched up his face. His nose grew into a long and pointed beak, his scales transformed into feathers – his arms became wings. He ruffled his feathers and made a throaty *"Craaw!"* before hopping onto Nona's shoulder. Nona flinched. Her head was still sore where he'd pecked her and pulled her hair all morning.

But Castor didn't peck or pull her hair now. He lowered his head and nuzzled against her cheek. The tiny feathers on the top of his head felt smooth and soft. Then he took off and landed in a flurry on the windowsill, cawed once more and was gone.

When Nona woke it was to the sound of things moving around downstairs. Lots of them.

Her blood ran cold. *Rattlesticks.* She sat up and looked around. Uncle Antoni's bed was empty.

Nona threw off the blanket and ran to the balcony. She hesitated, afraid to look over, but only for a second. Something drove her on: something stronger than fear. It was the urge to protect her uncle.

What she saw made her freeze. It wasn't the rattlesticks. The church was bustling full of people, all with her uncle's cartoons. Carrying sheets of glass. Preparing workspaces.

She couldn't believe her eyes.

There was something else too. All of them were working as if in a daze. They had to have been bewitched – like Uncle Antoni. *Alesea.*

Light streamed in through the glassless windows as Nona staggered down the stairs with her mouth open, rubbing her eyes. The dust danced around her in swirls, caught up in the movement of all these bodies. It must have been late morning, judging by the strong daylight and the birds in full-throated song outside.

Footsteps clopped past her, close by. "Uncle?" One look at him told Nona what she'd both suspected and feared: he was under Alesea's spell again and already back at work. But he also seemed to be directing the others, with silent points, taps on the shoulder and looks.

Her heart sank, remembering everything from last night. The rattlestick. The Soldier. Especially the Soldier. Should she find Alesea to let her know what had happened?

As it turned out, she didn't have to find Alesea at all.

The hare sat in the light from the doorway, its nose snuffling as it tasted Nona's scent on the air. Nona held her breath. "Alesea?"

In response, the hare hopped towards her across the intricately patterned tiled floor. Nona lost sight of it in the glare of light spilling from one of the windows, and it darted behind the branches of the sapling. But it was Alesea who emerged into view. She wore a long white dress with grass stains and sparkling silver embroidery at the hem, with bare feet poking out from beneath.

"Castor told me about your sight spell," Alesea said as she came closer, her tone as dark as her expression. "That you breathed the smoke and had an unwelcome visitor." She eyed the stone stairs, where a few bits of stick and root were still visible on the steps. Nona didn't have that same drained feeling as Alesea approached her this time. Not since she'd eaten the honey – and some of the food from the altar that she and Uncle Antoni had shared. The others didn't seem affected either. Had they eaten enchanted food too?

"It was an accident," said Nona. "I didn't mean to breathe in the smoke. No one told me I shouldn't—" She stopped herself. What if she'd got Castor into trouble by saying that? She hadn't thought. Her head felt muddied from another bad night's sleep. She'd seen the Soldier in her mind's eye all night – and found herself flying around the rafters again as a tiny bird.

Alesea didn't give anything away. Instead her face brightened in a smile, though she held Nona's gaze. "Of course it was an accident, my lovely. Of course. No one's blaming you. But it means we need to be extra cautious from now on." Alesea looked around. For a moment her shoulders relaxed. "It's going to be magnificent when it's finished, isn't it? Our sanctuary! Once it's complete it will be so powerful that one spell will seal it, and it will become impenetrable. You'll be safe inside. We all will."

Nona followed her gaze. It did have a certain atmosphere to it; a particularly pleasing quality of light. With her uncle's stained glass in place, it really would be magnificent.

The others – tradespeople she guessed – walked around and in between Nona and Alesea, busying themselves in silence. They'd laid out separate workstations now to cut glass on. If Uncle had worked alone the windows might've taken weeks, but with all this help the job should be finished in no time.

"I've brought in some helpers for your uncle," said Alesea, watching Nona. "Speed is of the essence, now more than ever, since he has seen you and been drawn to this place. We're lucky he doesn't yet know who you are, but he mustn't discover the umbrafell's importance before it's complete. He mustn't suspect our plan."

"They didn't have to be bewitched, though. Did they?" said Nona in a low voice. "All these people." Alesea's smile became tight, her eyes sharp as points.

"I told you," she said. "It is better this way. It's for everyone's safety."

"You don't like to be seen by humans, do you?" said Nona curiously. "Why?"

Alesea didn't answer, but said instead, "I mustn't stay long." She angled her head forwards so that her flower-adorned hair cascaded across her fur cape. "And neither must you. The Soldier must never suspect our connection to this place before it is built, and the magic sealed. So it's more important than ever that I'm not seen here, and that we are not seen together – by him, or any of his rattlesticks. Do you understand?"

Nona nodded. It felt as though she was being scolded by someone who was pretending not to be cross. She hated that. She'd rather someone just be angry with her and be done with it. At least that was honest.

Alesea raised her chin. "You must go to the woods," she said. "To stay with someone who can better protect you. Serafin, my spirit-sister. She will be able to teach you how to use your glimmer of magic in ... in ways I can't." Alesea momentarily looked away – but Nona didn't notice. Her mind was reeling about what leaving the church would mean.

"What about Uncle Antoni?" gasped Nona. She glanced at him, hunched over his sketches on the bench. She hated the idea of him coming out of his trance while she wasn't there. He would be confused without her to explain what was happening. Would he be frightened? For her? For himself? Her chest tightened. "No." She shook her head. "No, I can't. I won't go without my uncle."

"We need to get you your second skin as soon as possible," Alesea went on, gliding smoothly over Nona's panic. Her grey-green eyes sparkled. They were mesmerizing. Calming. The colour of moss-covered tombstones. Alesea stepped closer. Now Nona could see that the top part of Alesea's dress was embroidered all over in delicate gold flowers.

It reminded her of medieval patterns in some of the stained glass she'd helped restore – rendered in bright yellow silver stain. It was as if Alesea had stepped straight out of a stained-glass window herself.

A subtle numbness seemed to climb up Nona's neck and into her brain. An unspoken whisper hung around them, as if Alesea was speaking without moving her lips – in the way she had when they'd moved through the stone yesterday. She felt herself relax, her resolve begin to falter... Alesea was getting inside her head. Nona shook herself. "I won't leave Uncle Antoni," she said again through gritted teeth.

Alesea sighed sharply and stepped back. The numbness in Nona's body lifted instantly. Had Alesea just tried to persuade her with magic – and failed? Nona bristled.

"If you really care about your uncle then you must," Alesea snapped. "If you stay and you are seen again, you don't just jeopardize your own safety, but theirs too." She looked around at all the workers. At Uncle Antoni. "Your *uncle* included," she added.

Though Nona didn't want to accept it, she had to admit that what Alesea had said could be true. The rattlestick came too close to Uncle Antoni last night, and if more came... She had to go. Her shoulders sagged and tears rose into her eyes.

"Ohh, there, there," came Alesea's voice, soft and silky once more. "Once you have your second skin and some tutoring from Serafin, things will be a lot safer. And Castor will accompany you."

"But I'm human. How do I get a second skin?" Nona's voice came out hoarse through her tight throat.

Alesea smiled. "That will be for you to discover. No one else can do it for you. Now. Take this." Alesea bundled something smooth and cool into Nona's hand. When she looked at it, Nona saw it was a small, bluish stone.

"It's a pocketstone," Alesea said. "It's charged with my magic – similar to the illusion cast on the umbrafell to make it look derelict from the outside. But this spell won't last long. A day or two at the most. Keep it with you and it will create the illusion to his eye that you are a mere part of the landscape. But don't lose it or let it go," she continued. "And don't stay in the open too long. Because then he'll see what you really are."

With that, she backed away swiftly and was gone.

14

"No one else can do it for you," mimicked Castor. Once Alesea had left, he'd popped out from wherever he'd been hiding and started to complain. "Rubbish!" he went on. "She's the first to avoid getting her hands dirty."

Nona didn't say anything as she packed for their journey. She knew from her apprenticeship with Uncle that learning any craft involved hard work and patience. Of all the things Alesea had said, that was the part she didn't question. Besides, she was preoccupied with thoughts of leaving the umbrafell, and Uncle.

Castor was in his imp form today, the colour of glowing coals. And apparently not in the mood to stay still. He scuttled around her, clambering over the bag as she tried to pack it, mostly getting in the way. If Nona didn't distract him they'd never be ready to leave. Not that the thought of going didn't still fill her with dread.

"It's fine for Alesea to run away and hide, of course. Oh, yes," Castor went on. "But what about us? The least she could have done was come too. Isn't she worried about what might happen to m— to us?"

Nona stopped what she was doing, a loaf of bread half-wrapped in a cloth. The tone of Castor's voice had had an edge of real hurt in it. But why was he so upset? What exactly was Castor and Alesea's relationship? Then again, she supposed, if Alesea had been his only real company for years, it was no wonder if he felt abandoned. Yet something told Nona that wasn't all there was to it. She let the silence linger to see if it would draw him to explain.

"Never mind," mumbled Castor eventually, and continued to pace. Nona frowned, but let it go.

"What's this Serafin like, anyway?" she asked. She finished wrapping a loaf and rocked back on her heels. Castor unwrapped the bread again and pulled off a chunk to eat.

"What is there to know?" he said. "She's a spirit, like Alesea. They're a messed-up bunch, the spirits. Best to stay away from them altogether."

"Shame I don't have a choice," said Nona. "Anyway," she raised an eyebrow, "why don't you take your own advice, and stay away from Alesea?"

"It's different," said Castor, squirming and flashing electric yellow. "I owe her. And, besides, she's not so bad. You owe her too. For doing all this to protect you."

Nona frowned. Castor and Alesea clearly had a complicated, sticky web of a relationship.

"What about you?" Nona studied Castor as he stuffed more bread into his mouth. "Aren't you a spirit like them?" Castor stopped eating.

"Yes, and no," he said with his mouth full. "Not exactly like them."

"What kind of creature are you, if you don't mind me asking?" Nona hesitated before she asked the question and then wished she had kept quiet. Castor bristled in a wave of sharp silver points that ran from the top of his head to his tail, but said nothing. He clearly didn't want to tell her.

Perhaps it was like when people asked about her scar when they only were being nosy and not because they cared. Guilt sliced through her. She hadn't wanted to hurt him. "I'm sorry, Castor," she said. "I didn't mean—"

Castor waved his sticky-fingered hand. "It's OK. Anyway," he said, breadcrumbs flying out of his mouth, "hurry up and get packed. The sooner we set off the better." He gave her a wide grin, as if the last few seconds had never happened, which fell when he caught Nona's look. With exaggerated movements, he rewrapped Nona's loaf of bread.

Nona slipped a note telling Uncle Antoni where she'd gone onto the workbench in front of him and kissed his ice-cold cheek.

On second thought, Nona took a horseshoe nail – a long straight silver nail, which they usually used to keep the lead and cut glass in place while assembling a panel – and hammered it through the note. There. Now at least she wouldn't have to worry it would fall on the floor and get buried under paper.

She hesitated before leaving. *As long as we stick together, we'll be fine.* That's what he always told her. Now she was doing the exact opposite of sticking together. But what choice did she have?

Nona grabbed her bag and marched to the door where Castor waited. She tried to ignore the sick feeling sliding over her. "I'll be back soon, Uncle," she whispered. "I promise." Together she and Castor set out on their way.

The crisp morning air smelled like ice. Despite the glorious winter sunshine, a chill hung heavy around them – as well as within Nona. Neither of them, it turned out, knew the exact way to find Serafin. "I can't believe Alesea didn't give you a clue about where she's hidden Serafin's woods!" Castor raged. "She must've forgotten – *again*. Or she thinks I can remember the way. Which I can't." He paused. "Well, let's see if anything jogs my memory. It's definitely around here. Somewhere…" They had Nona's glass fragment at least. It had led them to Alesea. Maybe it would work for them this time too?

The protective stone Alesea had given her felt smooth and cool in Nona's pocket – almost as comforting as the half-heart glass. But its power wouldn't last long – and then she'd no longer be hidden from the Soldier. What then?

Nona tugged her scarf up around her ears and set off. Castor clambered up to her shoulder and transformed into a crow as they left the shadow of the umbrafell. "You're not going to start pecking me this time, are you?" she teased Castor.

"*Craaw.*"

"Why can't you be the other you, instead of a crow?" she asked out of curiosity. "I mean, it would make talking to each other much easier, wouldn't it?"

"Can't. Not safe," squawked Castor. Nona guessed his crow form must be Castor's disguise against the Soldier.

They made their way across the moors in the same direction as yesterday, in search of the same spirit path they had followed. Nona remembered how the path had split – how the woman in the golden shawl had left Alesea and headed over the moors. That had to be Serafin. And if they followed that branch of the spirit path, surely they would soon find her woods – and then her home.

They must have taken a wrong turn, though, because they went further and further and no spirit path appeared.

Every so often Castor would fly ahead and circle back, scanning the horizon, without success. He seemed as confused as Nona. It didn't matter how much she gazed into the half-heart glass. No visions of the past came to its surface.

Hunger and frustration finally got the better of them, and they stopped to eat some of their supplies, laying a blanket on the hard, icy ground. Or rather, Nona did, while Castor pecked and scratched at the earth, looking for beetles and worms. Little toadstools poked out between grass and leaves, and Nona wondered if adders might be slithering near by. She'd once read in a book that there were lots living in Dartmoor, but that they were very shy.

"Around here, should be," grumbled Castor,

continuing to scratch and peck at the ground. "Around here!"

The strength of the sun still hadn't warmed the earth, and a chill mist hung in the frost-fringed grass. Boggy puddles nearby stayed frozen into ridges and patterns at the edges, growing dense and gloopy at their centres. And although they were bathed in sunlight, the sky was thick with cloud.

Nona finished her food and lay down on the blanket.

"Close now," Castor squawked. "Must be." He ruffled his feathers and took off, no doubt to scout for Serafin's woods.

Nona ran her fingers over the half-heart glass again. Maybe it wasn't properly charged with magic – light energy, according to Alesea. She'd said her half-heart stored it. Wasn't that how the Soldier's glass heart worked too? Back at Uncle's studio she'd kept hers on the windowsill to see it shine.

Perhaps the problem was that she wasn't reading it right. Could she read it now, if she really tried? She closed her eyes, resting her precious glass fragment against her chest and touching it lightly with her fingers. After so many disturbed nights she was tired and drained. It would be easy to let herself drift off. But instead she focused on the glass.

Its energy warmed her fingers in an instant. Just as it had at the studio the first night she saw Alesea, and the many times she'd instinctively used it before, without really understanding how it worked or what it did. A tingling warmth climbed up her fingers, her wrists, her arms. When she closed her eyes she could see the pink glow...

An image emerged. Suddenly Nona was looking down at herself from above. She was lying on the blanket with the glass on her chest. The image of her grew smaller as the viewpoint rose upwards, showing more of their surroundings: the rolling moor with a large hill to the north. And now she really looked, something wasn't right about the hill. It became transparent, faded, and where it had once been was a wood.

That must be it! That must be where the woods were hidden. She should get up, flag down Castor to tell him. But the image quickly changed. Now Nona saw her uncle's studio: their home, crawling with rattlesticks. They roamed around workbenches. Crept up and down the stairs. Peered into the bedrooms. Was this real? How had they found where she lived so quickly? Did this mean the Soldier finally knew who she was? Nona stifled a cry, but kept her eyes closed. She could feel there was more to see.

The pinkish darkness of her eyelids began to move again, to shift, forming the now-familiar shape of the Soldier. Nona's lungs tightened in panic. She could see the red glow in his chest, brighter than ever. And his eyes, staring out from behind a stag skull. This time she heard his voice. It was loud and clear, as if spoken into her ear. *Where are you, little mouse? You can't hide for long.*

Nona jerked upright, sending Castor flying back in a flurry. He must have returned already from his scouting mission. "What is it?" he flapped.

For a moment Nona couldn't answer. Then she said breathlessly, "I know where we have to go. Over ... there." She found the hill with ease and pointed it out across the rolling landscape. "But, Castor, that's not all I saw. The rattlesticks. At Uncle's house! And the Soldier – he spoke to me just now in my head. I think he must have sensed me using the glass." There was no doubt in her mind that these had been visions of something real – not her own imaginings. It had all been so detailed.

In two quick hops, Castor backed away, his head cocked to the side. "His magic. Getting stronger. Must be," was all he said.

"Castor," said Nona. "What if he finds me? What if—"

"All right, stop it." Castor transformed into an imp but tucked his hand into Nona's pocket so that he touched the stone. It was a weird thing to do – but Nona guessed that by touching it, it would keep him hidden too. "I know you've got Alesea's pocketstone," Castor said, "but you need your second skin now too."

Nona looked at him in horror. "I've already told you," she said. "I am not letting you stick leaves on my face."

"Forget the leaves!" Castor hissed back. "I mean you, learning to properly transform, now. Depends, though," he added.

"On what?"

"On you. Whether you're ready."

Nona shrugged her shoulders. "How will I even know unless I try?"

With his body in a sort of awkward crouch and his round eyes focused on Nona, Castor looked a little like a panther waiting to pounce. Despite the situation, the thought made Nona smirk.

Castor scowled. "Stop it," he said. "It's not funny." He glanced over his shoulder. Nona could hardly believe that Castor was suddenly being the sensible one.

"The way to do it is to make an item of clothing. It has to be something deeply special. Or," he went on quickly, seeing Nona's look of disbelief, "if you're not in a position to do that, like now, obviously, well, then you choose something you've got on. Like that tatty old jumper of yours."

"Tatty!" shrieked Nona. "I'll have you know I love this jumper. It's … it *was* my brother's."

"Good," said Castor, leaping up, only to shoot his hand back into Nona's pocket just as quickly. "Good," he repeated in a whisper. "If it's something you love there's more chance of this working. Now. Close your eyes. Feel the jumper all around you. Feel its warmth. Feel it *becoming* you."

"This is real magic," said Nona. "What if I can't do it?"

Castor raised an eyebrow and smiled. "You can see spirit paths, can't you? And spirits. I'd say you can grow a second skin if you concentrate."

That was all true – about the spirit paths, the spirits. It had actually been playing on her mind a lot recently. Why was it that she could see these things when other humans didn't seem to – with her own eyes, and not just with the power absorbed by her half-heart? In fact, why was it that she could use the half-heart in the way she did at all? Was it why the Soldier was after *her*? Nona took a deep breath and closed her eyes. She focused on the jumper, as Castor had instructed. On its softness. Its warmth. The way it rested over her body.

She imagined the yarn of it fusing with her skin.

Her whole body tingled. As if she was filled with an excitement she could hardly contain. As if her body was poised, ready to do somersaults, or backflips – or anything she could dream of.

"That's it," came Castor's voice. He sounded far away. "Now think of an animal. Anything that doesn't stand out. Not an elephant or a giraffe, obviously. More like a fox, for example, or a hare, like Alesea. Preferably something *fast*."

A hare? Nona loved hares, but she'd never felt any real urge to be one. And yet, to be able to fly... That was different. Sometimes Uncle Antoni would begin to tell her what it was like, being in his plane during the war, before he went quiet and changed the subject. She lived for those stories. The tiny houses below. The twinkling lights...

Her uncle's nickname for her flitted through her head. Jenny Wren. And those dreams she'd had of flying around the church...

And then she was falling and shrinking at the same time. She put out her arms to steady herself, and instead of arms, she found wings. And instead of balancing, she was flying.

15

It was exactly as Nona had dreamed it. Her wings worked fast and effortlessly. It was second nature. All she had to do was think about it and she would zip from one spot to another. All she could feel was the thrill of being in the air. She rocketed skywards, swooped this way and that. Inside her mind she screamed with joy – but from her mouth poured the warbles and chirps of a wren.

The world from up high looked much more beautiful. There were no streets and houses here, but networks of streams and jutting rock, hills, valleys and tors, the green and umber of the land rising through pale mist, the scars of ancient settlements. Nona didn't just feel like she was seeing it – she felt *part* of it.

Her heart welled with wonder. This was real magic – and *she'd* done it.

Castor – a crow – joined her in flight. He weaved and glided around her. Then drifted further away, cawing. Nona followed – towards the hill under which Serafin's woods were hidden. It had a shimmering transparency at the edges, as if light didn't fall across it in the same way as everywhere else. She could see that now.

Together they flew towards it, the illusion of the hill rippling around them like a heat haze the closer they came, until it vanished altogether. In its place stood a lush, green wood. The sight of it filled Nona with awe. Nona scanned the ground in search of a house that could be Serafin's – she guessed that's what Castor was doing too – but the trees were too dense to see anything from above. Perhaps they would have better luck on the ground.

Nona came back to earth. She barely had to think twice about becoming human again and there she was – clothes, rucksack and all. Nona beamed. Even now she tingled all over with the thrill of having been a wren.

The atmosphere among the trees, however, was very different from in the skies.

Castor landed on her shoulder, gripping tight. The breeze had died away into an eerie stillness. The temperature dropped. The smell of the frost and fields gave way to a scent of leaves and woodland growth. All was still and quiet, but for the odd cracks and clunks of who knew what: scuttling creatures, or nuts falling through branches and onto the carpeted ground. Or rattlesticks? Nona shivered, and not just with the cold. Couldn't they only come out at night? No. *At night or in shadowy places*, Castor had said. Well, this was definitely a shadowy place. She drew her scarf around her chin again and tried to ignore the dread in the pit of her stomach.

Castor ruffled his feathers and shuffled. He was clearly nervous. Another creak came from Nona's left and sent her heart racing. Had a rattlestick seen them land? Had they seen Nona transform?

"Arm yourself," squawked Castor. His crow-voice sounded deeper and more serious than ever. He hopped to the floor, scratched at it, and then drew his wing out in a strange, awkward way to cover the earth. When he withdrew it, a small pile of stones had appeared – just as in the umbrafell. Nona stuffed some in her pocket. "Rattlesticks won't be able to see us because of the pocketstone, though … right, Castor?" Nona said.

"Soldier can't. Sticks can," replied Castor.

Ahead of them came another creaking sound – and the clacking of stone against stone. Nona's blood ran cold. This wasn't good.

Almost without thinking about it, Nona felt herself begin to transform into a wren. But Castor's harsh and urgent voice snapped her out of it. "Not here. Not safe. Sticks watching." Of course. If they saw her transform, that would be her disguise revealed, and she'd only just gained her second skin. She'd have to hope they hadn't seen her when she first landed.

Nona changed her direction and clambered over moss-covered rocks, some of which grew in strange, geometric patterns and swirls. Searching for something – anything – that she could use to defend herself if she needed to. The creaking, clicking sounds were all around now. Nona ducked under a wizened tree that had grown into a kind of archway. The woods were denser here, with patches of black mud around. Bogs, she realized. She found a large stick, a fallen branch, and grabbed it tight with both hands.

The first rattlestick appeared from behind a tree ahead of them, bone white and hollow-eyed.

16

Two more rattlesticks stepped from behind the trees, just beyond the patch of bog. Scouts, by the look of it – maybe lost, or roaming around looking for anything suspicious. Castor shrieked and flapped on Nona's shoulder. She tightened her grip around the branch. Two thin arms rose out of the bog, scrabbling to lift itself out, another rattlestick, still forming, wiry bits of dead roots and old stones attaching themselves to the body as if by some magnetic force.

Nona inched back before she heard something that made her stop dead. They were behind her too. She was surrounded. The rattlesticks in front formed a circle and began to move in.

"What do you want?" shouted Nona, her eyes scanning for an escape route. "I haven't got anything for you except a smack on the head." She waved her branch, but her voice came out strained and frightened. Were *all* the woods around here crawling with rattlesticks, attacking anything that got in their way?

One of the rattlesticks clacked its jaws but they didn't stop moving closer.

Castor launched himself from Nona's shoulder. In one swift movement, he swooped down, grabbed a large rock in his claws and zoomed upwards, letting the rock go above the rattlestick that had crawled out of the bog. The rock arced through the air and smashed into the creature's ribs. Pieces of it scattered across the ground. Its lower half walked another couple of paces before Nona jabbed it with her stick and it fell apart.

Nona took her chance and ran through the gap it had made – out of the circle of rattlesticks. But more emerged from behind the trees ahead, and those she'd left behind turned to follow – encircling her again.

High in the treetops, Castor cawed. His voice echoed through the trees. What was he doing up there?

Sweat prickled in Nona's hairline. What were her options? She had to think. If one touch was all it would take to turn her into a rattlestick, she couldn't risk dodging between them. They would be waiting for that. All the games of tag she'd ever played with the kids on her old street told her that – and only her brother could ever beat her at it. What else? Could she climb a tree? Tree climbing, as a city child, was not her thing. If only she could transform into a wren… But that would give away her disguise, as well as the fact that she could do spirit magic. No. That had to be a last resort.

The only option left was to fight.

"Stay back," warned Nona, swishing her branch. She took a small step backwards herself, and then another. Bone thin fingers picked through her hair.

Nona shrieked and spun around. It had been a tree branch – that's all. Her heart thudded in her chest as if it wanted to break free from her body. One of the rattlesticks that had been drawing in behind her moved its jaw up and down in a way that looked like a cackle – though the only sound it made was more strange creaking, like the bough of a tree blown in a gale. A strange, emotionless mockery.

That was it. She wasn't going to stand here and be laughed at. Nona pulled one of the rocks Castor had conjured earlier from her pocket and hurled it at the laughing rattlestick.

She aimed for its head, but she misjudged the weight of her rock. Instead the rock sailed downwards faster than she'd expected and barrelled into the creature's pelvis. The whole rattlestick crumpled inwards in a shower of old sticks.

"Craaw!" called Castor, his voice echoing again over the trees. Nona swung round in time to see more rattlesticks rising from the bog. And one of the others heading straight for her, only paces away. It must have seized its chance to advance when she wasn't looking. They weren't smart – but they were sneaky.

An object came crashing through the trees. A chestnut, perhaps – though it was clear who had dropped it: Castor. It clunked the rattlestick coming at Nona directly on the top of the head with a hollow *thunk*. But the rattlestick carried on striding closer.

Now, however, it was in range of Nona's branch.

With a yell, Nona thrust it into the rattlestick's chest like a soldier's bayonet. As the rattlestick crumbled, it swiped at Nona with its arm. She jerked back just in time. Its fingers whistled through the air past her nose. She felt the breeze of it against her cheek. Nona gasped at the close call, but there was no time to rest. Her mind raced, trying to keep track of the numbers and their positions. Four in front, three behind – no! Six, plus another two to the sides… It was impossible to order her thoughts. To keep note of them all.

With another urgent *"Craaw!"* Castor took off from the trees. Nona could see his shadow disappearing. Was he leaving her again?

"Castor," she cried. "Castor, come back!" But she couldn't afford to take her eyes off the advancing rattlesticks.

Nona delved into her pocket. Only one rock left, and so many rattlesticks... She'd have to make it count. Nona took aim at the one closest. Drew back her arm ready to throw. But just as she'd launched it, a *swish*, *thwack* and *clatter* came from behind. Nona's throw faltered. Her rock took out just one of the rattlestick's legs. Although it fell to the floor, its top half remained whole.

Nona spun around to see what had made the noise, and had to shield her eyes from the most dazzling light she'd ever seen. Rattlestick parts sprayed across the ground, many rolling to a stop at her feet. As her eyes adjusted to the painful brightness, Nona saw a tall, dark-haired woman in a sparkling golden shawl embroidered like bird's wings standing in the rattlestick's place. And Castor, sleek black and magnificent, perched on her shoulder.

Serafin. It had to be.

The woman held a tall wooden staff at a right angle to her body. It's what she must have smashed the rattlestick with, because as Nona gaped at her, the woman plunged it into the chest of a second. This one hissed as it disintegrated. Smoke rose from its sticks and stones – its falling parts. Whatever the staff was made of, or enchanted with, it had clearly been designed with destroying rattlesticks in mind.

Nona was mesmerized by the woman. Her grip on her own branch loosened. She didn't know if it was the glittering of her shawl, or the strength and assuredness of her movements, but this woman seemed to give off a radiant, sun-like energy.

Serafin met Nona's gaze, and her expression changed. "Look out!" she cried. Castor opened his wings and cawed. In a split-second Serafin charged at Nona and thrust her staff at Nona's feet. There was a clatter and a hiss, and Nona looked down in time to see the top half of the rattlestick she'd partially destroyed fall to bits.

17

NONA STARED AT THE MESS OF ROOTS AND ROCKS that, seconds earlier, had been a rattlestick. It had been so close to touching her. So close to turning Nona into one of them. She could hardly fathom it.

With a huge sigh of relief, Nona looked into the face of her rescuer.

Serafin stared back, cold and hard. "What are you doing here, putting yourselves and me at risk like that?" she said. "Even hidden with magic, this wood is rife with these creatures. You are supposed to be keeping out of harm's way at the umbrafell. Castor! Explain."

Castor squawked and left Serafin's shoulder in a hurry, landing heavily on Nona's.

"And you," said Serafin, not waiting for an answer but returning her piercing stare to Nona. "What do you call that display? How do you ever expect to face the Soldier like that?"

Face the Soldier? Nona's mind reeled in confusion and horror. What did Serafin mean? She was supposed to be hiding from the Soldier – protected by the magic of the umbrafell – not *fighting* him. But Serafin had stalked away, not waiting for a response. She took something out of her shawl – what looked like a small phial – and scattered its contents over the nearest bogs. They began to hiss and steam as the liquid touched them. "This should prevent any others rising – for a short time at least," she muttered as she worked.

Nona watched Serafin in silence. Her ears felt like they were burning, and her knees had begun to tremble. A mix of fear and shame curdled in her stomach.

Once Serafin had finished her task, she marched back towards Nona.

Nona had to shield her eyes from the glare of Serafin's golden birdwing shawl as it caught the light. The spirit wore a silky, turquoise tunic over loose trousers and, closer up, Nona could see that her near-black hair was streaked with delicate strands of silver. Tracing up the inside of one slender brown arm snaked a paler brown pattern of ferns. Nona admired the marking straight away for its curves and lines.

It took her a moment to realize it was a scar.

All Nona could hear was the drumming of her own heart, the rushing of blood in her head. Her mouth had dried up, taking her ability to speak.

"I take it from your silence," said Serafin, "that you didn't know of this. No doubt Alesea believes she's been protecting you by keeping it from you. Or herself." She raised an eyebrow and glared first at Nona, then Castor. Castor made a low rumbling noise in his throat and hung his beak. Nona still couldn't speak at all. She was trembling all over.

Serafin's glare, Nona's mistake with the rattlestick: it all made Nona feel small, and pathetic, and ashamed. It felt as if Serafin could see right through her – and could see nothing but weakness.

But she wasn't weak. She was fast, and smart, she listened and learned, and she had Uncle Antoni and now a friend in Castor, and she tried hard. Nona took a deep breath and raised her chin. She might be just a child but she'd survived this far. She held Serafin's gaze.

Something flickered across Serafin's eyes and she seemed to soften. It was an odd look. It reminded her of the way Alesea had studied Nona when they'd first met. A kind of recognition. As if they'd met before.

"Alesea sent us here to find you," Nona said, in as

strong a voice as she could muster. "You are Serafin, aren't you?"

Serafin huffed. "What do you think?" she said. Although her tone was gentle, and Nona thought that even the ghost of a smile curled her lips.

"We had to come," Nona went on, "because the umbrafell isn't safe any longer. Not until the windows are complete."

"And you think you'll be safer here with me?" Serafin threw her head back and laughed, but it was totally without mirth. "Alesea should never have sent you. She's put you in danger. I have enough of those things to deal with as it is." She gestured at the rattlesticks scattered across the ground.

"Please," said Nona. She couldn't stop thinking about what Serafin had said. "What do you mean, that I'm to face the Soldier?" Her limbs felt heavy with confusion and exhaustion now. "All I know is that he's looking for me. That he wants to sacrifice me and bring his son back to life. I don't even know why it's me he wants! No one's telling me anything. I—"

Serafin rested her hand on Nona's shoulder and warmth exploded from her palm. Nona gasped. It warmed her blood, strengthened her resolve. "Less of that," said Serafin, not unkindly. "Come with me and I'll explain as much as I can. But we will need to work quickly. As I said, there will be an attack tonight, and I must be ready. Preparing the defences is the least either of you can do. I've lost time because of you."

Nona stared at Serafin. In spite of the harshness of her words, the warmth that radiated from her was comforting. Nona found herself trusting her. She was at least, it seemed, honest.

The spirit beckoned for Nona and Castor to follow her, but she didn't wait for them. She set off marching among the trees.

Serafin led them along a twisted path through the woods, until one side dropped away into a thick, black bog. The path sloped down through an arched open doorway along a series of steps formed from roots and well-trodden soil, leading past lush flowers and plants. Then through another doorway, this one set within a red brick wall covered mostly with ivy, and a wooden door that finished in a point at the very top. It was certainly well concealed, this house, Nona thought. Not even the telltale lights of the spirit paths shone here, aside from those that trailed Serafin, burning up seconds after they'd appeared. But then Alesea had hinted that she could hide some of the lights, as she had the woods.

"Castor," began Nona as they walked. "What Serafin said, about me facing the Soldier. Did you—"

Castor squawked. "Didn't know," he said. He nuzzled her cheek.

Tears rose in Nona's eyes. "What do you think it means?" she asked. But Castor said no more. Deep down, she already knew.

Beyond the second door, Nona caught her first glimpse of Serafin's home. She gasped at the mill house with flowers climbing up the walls to a thatched roof, and a large mill wheel slowly turning over a stream that ran beneath it. It was beautiful.

On this side of the wall, plants of every sort grew, with a multitude of coloured flowers and berries crammed together in one luscious place. Spirit lights *did* shine here, not in straight lines but all around the garden that Serafin must regularly weave through.

Nona longed to pull out her sketchbook: it would all make a wonderful panel for a stained-glass window. Uncle Antoni would love to see it too, to draw it, to capture its beauty in glass.

Pain tugged at Nona's heart at the thought of him alone in the church. What if the Soldier had sent more rattlesticks to the umbrafell? What if he'd already been touched? The thought pulled at her as she and Castor followed Serafin's path through the door.

Inside it smelled of dried herbs and flowers. Serafin sat at a small table, crushing seeds in a pestle and mortar. In the corner was a porcelain sink with tiny turquoise tiles between it and the window ledge. The walls were lined with shelves, and on the shelves sat row upon row of neat, wooden pots, and what looked like crystal phials.

This was a working home, like Uncle's studio. Only a million times tidier.

Nona gazed at the pots on the shelves. Each one was labelled something different: *Pettigrain, Snakestongue, Laburnum.*

"You may sit," said Serafin, nodding towards the chair opposite her.

Nona stayed on her feet. "No," she said. "I want to know what you meant about facing the Soldier."

18

SERAFIN STOPPED WORKING AND FIXED NONA with another scornful look. Nona's stomach flipped. But, as in the woods, Nona thought she saw recognition in the spirit's gaze – and this time maybe even a little dread.

Serafin sighed. "I'll tell you – *if* you think you can handle it," she said, raising an eyebrow. "Alesea may have been right to keep it from you. You are a child, after all, as she likes to point out."

"Maybe I am," said Nona sharply, "but if it's something about me, and it affects me, then I think I should hear it." She folded her arms. Castor made a rumbling noise and glided towards the sink. Something told her he was afraid of how Serafin might react and had decided to get out of the way.

But Serafin remained still – and serious. "Very

well," she said, straightening in her seat. "To protect you within the umbrafell's walls *is* our plan – but not all of it. It's important to keep you safe, now more than ever—"

"Because the Soldier wants to kill me," interrupted Nona. She couldn't help it: her voice cracked slightly as she said this. Serafin nodded slowly.

"In order to resurrect his own son. But to reorder nature like that, life must be given for a life. He can only do that when he has your glass to make his power strong enough. Your own shard of magic," Serafin added. "Which is why we must keep you – and it – safe."

"But why *my* life?" Nona could feel hot tears prickling her eyes.

"That I can't tell you," said Serafin. "Not yet. In order to hear the truth we must be ready for it. And, strong-willed as you are, Nona, as you've always been..." Serafin's mouth twitched, "you are not yet ready."

Nona gritted her teeth in frustration, but Serafin remained resolute.

"Would you rather it was someone else's life the Soldier needed?" Serafin said, tilting her head. "Would that be any better?"

"No, of course not. That's not what I—" Of

course Nona didn't want that. Why did any life have to be sacrificed at all?

"You are the key to defeating the Soldier for good, Nona," Serafin said firmly. "The Soldier won't stop at bringing his son back. He's power-hungry now. He's been waging a war on spirits since the day he learned of us and it won't be long before he brings his wrath to humans too. He thinks of himself as superior – that his luck is owed to him and not luck at all, but merely proof of his superiority, and by the same token, the misfortune of others is weakness. Deserved. He'll turn everything living into rattlesticks unless he's stopped. Alesea and I have foreseen it.

"You are the only one who can stop the Soldier," Serafin went on. "By taking his power. By breaking his glass heart. But if you face him now, before you're ready?" Serafin paused and her face softened. "Then you will fail, child. Alesea and I have foreseen that too." Fine lines, like the most delicate of leaf veins, blossomed around her eyes in a sudden burst of sympathy.

A heavy silence filled the room while Nona absorbed all this. Break the Soldier's glass heart? Her? Memories of splintering glass filled her head before she could block them out – the stench of dust and fire. Her stomach turned.

"But how do you know I'm the one?" said Nona. "Not even the Soldier knows. Are you *sure*?"

Serafin nodded. "We've pieced our predictions together through snatches of magic: whispers from the life and light around us. It's never certain. But we're as sure as we can be." She didn't explain further.

"Why me, though?' said Nona quietly. "You said yourself that I'm not ready."

"No spirit can touch the heart," said Serafin simply. "Nor can any other human except you. That's why we must protect you in the umbrafell. Until you are … capable."

"You mean until I'm older," snapped Nona. "How long do you expect to keep me there anyway? I can't stay for ever. My uncle and I have got lives – and there's the studio to run." She frowned.

"No, I do not mean 'until you're older'," said Serafin, ignoring Nona's second question. "I mean what I said." Her energy, which filled the room in a way Nona could only explain as a pressure, seemed to grow more intense. Nona found her legs trembling under Serafin's glare. "And what I said was," Serafin went on, "*until you are more capable.*" The force of Serafin's energy subsided. Her tone softened again. "Now," she said. "The least you can do is show a willingness to *learn*. These leaves need to be picked off and put into there." Serafin pointed to a large bowl by her feet.

Alesea had told her that Serafin would be able to teach Nona about magic – in ways that Alesea herself couldn't. Was this it? Nona was starting to like Serafin's way – stern, perhaps, but fair and trustworthy. She reminded her a bit of Uncle. Slowly, Nona took a seat opposite Serafin and started pulling off the small, fuzzy leaves from a clipping of the plant. She breathed the scent deeply. They smelled lemony. Out of the corner of her eye she thought she caught Serafin smile.

Once Castor had finished skulking around the shelves, he came over to help. Nona studied Serafin's hands as they worked the pestle and mortar. There was the fern-like scar again, snaking up her arm. Nona realized then that Serafin hadn't once looked twice at her own.

"It's my lightning scar," said Serafin, making Nona jump. "I'm proud of this one. It took a lot for me to get it and was in exchange for some highly desirable magic." Serafin smiled even more broadly. "If you were wondering, that is."

Nona flushed, and knew that her own scar must surely be more visible against her reddening cheeks.

Beside the bowl into which the picked leaves went was a bucket filled with water.

"What's that for?" asked Nona, pointing at the bucket.

"You mustn't touch it," said Serafin sharply. "The water is from a forbidden place close by in these woods, a cursed, bottomless lake. It reflects terrible truths from the past – and sometimes the future. Even the touch of it can cause visions. For some, it can kill. It destroys the rattlesticks, who finally see themselves for what they really are: dead things." Nona was mesmerized. Nothing is more alluring than the thing you're told not to touch. Everyone knows that.

"The leaves are for spell pouches," Serafin went on. "These will create a mist to confuse the rattlesticks. The more we can send back into the bog as soon as they've risen, the better. I'll admit, it makes a change to have some companionship as I do this," she added, her tone suddenly conversational. "It has been only Alesea and I for so long. And if she were to come here now we would face twice the rattlesticks, besides which her magic can do little against them. Her power works on humans – not those empty things. So we must stay apart." Nona stared at Serafin. The powerful spirit looked weary and sad.

They worked on into the evening, first preparing the dried plants, then putting them into pouches. Serafin took her large staff of gnarled wood and anointed the head of it with the water. They did the same with Nona's branch – the one she'd picked up in the woods – carefully.

"You need to begin learning how to defend yourself," said Serafin with a steady look, "so you may as well start tonight. Although I expect you to stay back and let Castor and I deal with the rattlesticks. Your job is to observe. But, should you need it, this will be your weapon." Serafin handed her the branch. "Keep it close at all times. Press it against a rattlestick, and they will crumble into their true form. Do not touch the anointed end yourself."

Nona wondered why it was all right for Serafin to touch the water and not her. But Serafin was a spirit after all. Perhaps it was because of her power.

All the while the mill wheel of Serafin's house clunked and groaned and creaked as it turned, in a soothing rhythm that accompanied their preparations. But as their work was completed, and the encroaching dusk forced them to light candles, the relentless sound of the mill wheel lulled Nona less. It became a noise that marked the passing of time – each second counting down to nightfall, when Serafin told them the rattlesticks would return.

"I must warn you," said Serafin as they retreated to the other rooms, to rest before the battle. "These rattlesticks will be ... different to the ones you're used to. They come to steal magic – from me, and from what I harvest from the mill's water and my garden. It's the world's magic, really, of which I am a custodian. And they do so to give it to the Soldier. These rattlesticks wear darkness like a disguise. They... trick the eye and the ear. You must not listen."

Nona nodded solemnly. She supressed a yawn and her eyes watered, and yet she could see how much more tired Serafin looked now in the candlelight. It wasn't simply the dark shadows under her eyes – although they were there. It was a weariness that went to the bone, fighting against her own limbs, slowing every action until it seemed she was moving underwater. How long had Serafin been doing this? Fighting in these woods, alone?

Serafin showed Nona to a bed before settling herself down in a rocking chair and snuffing out the light. The bed was comfortable, but Nona couldn't sleep. The more she turned Serafin's words over in her mind, the more the fear inside her churned, like the water of the mill wheel.

She reached out for the half-heart, over on the nearby bedside table. Her fingers found its cool surface in the dark, and the tips of them tingled. Grew warmer. Then hotter. "Show me Uncle Antoni," she whispered. "I need to know he's safe." She kept her voice low so as not to disturb the others. Castor was an imp and already curled up like a cat near her feet, snoring slightly. Serafin was silent. Nona couldn't tell if she was asleep or awake.

Nona closed her eyes as she felt the heat from the glass travel up her arm as it always did. Waited for the shapes to emerge from the pink glow in her mind.

But it wasn't Uncle she saw. It was a group of men sitting around the dining table of what looked like a country house with lace curtains, a grand old working fireplace and a carved wooden cabinet filled with dishes, cups and plates. The men wore the woollen khaki tunics of the Great War, and supposedly the last. They were all British officers, judging by their badges. In a civilian home, they looked totally out of place.

Nona frowned. Why was she seeing this? She tried to focus on her uncle again. But the image persisted.

A banner hung above the fireplace, which read: *Hautmont est libéré*, and a couple who might have been the owners of the house hurried around the men at the table, filling their large cups made of beautiful red pressed glass – glass that would have been pushed into a mould when it was molten to give it its intricate relief patterns. Nona knew only a little French but she knew that Hautmont must be the name of the town, and it had been liberated.

This was a celebration of some sort. A successful mission to take the French town back from German occupation?

Nona's attention turned to one of the officers. He was younger than the others – much younger. Surely too young to be in the army at all... Though she'd heard of boys signing up for the war, especially when they'd believed the fighting would be over in a matter of months, and not the years of horror that really took place. She studied him hard, her forehead aching with the effort. His youth wasn't the only thing that made him stand out. There was a confidence – a swagger – about the others that he didn't have.

It didn't take much for Nona to spot an odd one out like her. She'd bet anything that the others had been officers from the very start, owing to their family's wealth or status. Whereas *he* had been promoted. Probably by someone in that room.

As she watched, the young officer lifted the red glass to his lips, and froze, staring into the glass. No – *through* it. He was staring straight at her. Nona held back a scream. Still he kept his gaze fixed on her. There was a movement – a reflection – in the glass itself. A flash of honey-coloured hair. Then the man shouted, "Stop!"

Nona opened her eyes and lay rigid in bed. That voice… It was unmistakably the Soldier's. She recognized it from her vision on the moors when he'd called her "little mouse". And the reflection in the pressed glass. She was sure it was Alesea's. Had she just seen the Soldier when he was no more than a man?

Nona lay in the bed, shivering, wondering what it all meant – until an uneasy sleep finally rose up and claimed her.

19

FOR A MOMENT NONA HAD NO IDEA WHERE SHE was, or what was happening. Nightfall had come, that much was clear from the darkness pierced only by steadily burning lamps. A downpour had come with it, judging by the clattering on the ceiling.

Then Nona remembered it all. The woods. Serafin. The rattlesticks. Her heart sank.

Serafin was already awake and sitting upright in a chair, her staff across her knees like a defensive barrier. Dappled moonlight shimmied over her, but otherwise she was still. Listening to sounds that Nona herself couldn't hear, behind the cacophony of rainfall.

"This rain will make the lake water less effective," she murmured, as if to herself. "But it will at least make the bog more lethal. Either way, our only option is to fight. We can't wait for them to breach the walls or steal any more power than they already have."

She fixed Nona with her steady gaze, and Nona was taken aback by the strength in it – the courage. "Are you ready?" Serafin asked.

Nona didn't feel ready. She felt drained. Waking from sleep at such an unusual time had made her cold and shivery, despite the warmth of the room. Not to mention the fear that burned inside her gut. But there was no use in saying so: she *had* to be ready.

Nona pulled back the covers and sat up to put on her shoes. Serafin gave a nod, stood up herself and shook out her hair, her staff clutched firmly in one hand. Nona reached for her own stick. Then, thinking about it, she took the glass fragment from her pocket and slipped it under the pillow. Best to leave it here where it would be safe. The pocketstone, however, she kept with her. It would hide her from the Soldier, if not his rattlesticks.

With a *"Craaw!"* that told her Castor had transformed, he glided onto Nona's shoulder. She liked him there, she'd found. His weight felt familiar now. And heartening. Yet her thoughts couldn't help returning to Uncle Antoni. She hoped he was safe and warm in his bed in the company of dreams. Not fretting for her. Not visited by any more rattlesticks...

Please let him be asleep, she said to herself. *And let him be safe*. She tried hard to push her worry away, to stop it leading to panic. She mustn't be distracted.

Outside, the cold, damp air with its smell of churned mud and leaves hit Nona like a wall and sharpened her senses. The rain plummeted through the trees and onto the ground like a hail of gunfire as they made their way down the steps that led to the first door. The river that ran beside them was swollen, with water gushing past the mill wheel attached to Serafin's house, making it spin so fast that its rhythmic groans, creaks and clunks were one long, ear-piercing screech.

Nona took a deep breath as she walked at Serafin's shoulder. She had to stay calm. But try telling that to her body. Already she could feel the cold sweat mixed with rain on her back, the memory of the smell of burning clouding her senses.

"It's best not to let them get close," Serafin told Nona, without looking round. "We'll use the mist to confuse them. Make them stumble back into the bog. That way we don't have to look at them: see their stolen faces or listen to their trick words up close." This time, she did look down at Nona. "The ones who don't fall into the bog will keep coming. So don't listen to them or believe any of the things they tell you. Remember: they aren't who they pretend to be and the things they say to you aren't true. They're only designed to make you give in. To give up." She pursed her lips. "What must you not do, Nona?"

"I mustn't give in," replied Nona, her voice hoarse. "Or give up."

"Precisely." Serafin turned away to survey the dark wood ahead – the sweep of path, all knotted with tree roots. And beside it, the deep, thick bog. Nona squinted into the darkness and hoped her eyes would grow accustomed to it soon.

All at once the rain eased and then stopped altogether, leaving an eerie silence.

"*Craaw!*" Still perched on her shoulder, Castor stretched out his wings to their full extent. His gaze was fixed dead ahead. Her heart pounding, Nona followed his line of sight and went completely cold at what she saw. The outline of a crowd of skeleton-like creatures, pearl white and stick-thin, shuffling along the path. There had to be fifty of them at least.

A gasp escaped Serafin. "There've never been this many before," she said. "Not in one night. I'll do my best to stop them, Nona, but you may have to fight too. Be prepared."

The creatures surged towards them. Nona's legs felt rooted to the spot, and her teeth had started chattering with fear. If she'd been able to move, she might've fled back to the house. But that, and knowing Serafin would defend them, gave her a drop of courage.

In one swift motion, Serafin dug her fingers into the pouch she carried, flung the herbs they'd prepared into the air and muttered some words. A bank of mist rose around the rattlesticks and engulfed them. All Nona could hear were creaks and clatters and groans. Did this mean it had worked? Was that the noise of many rattlesticks tumbling back into the sticky depths of the bog, in pieces? She hoped so. Castor shifted his weight on her shoulder.

Nona held her breath and waited.

One by one, the remaining rattlesticks appeared out of the mist. Two. Five. Ten. More. Serafin's magic hadn't been as effective as they'd hoped. Nona couldn't keep count now. She tightened her grip on the stick. If only her hands weren't sweating so much – and shaking...

She heard a familiar voice calling her name. Uncle Antoni. Was he here? But how— Then she realized. It came from one of the rattlesticks. Nona's mouth dropped open when she saw it. The mist Serafin had created clung a little to its face, giving the creature almost human features.

The face was Uncle Antoni's too.

"My little Nona!" the rattlestick said. "Come to me. Let me hold you, take care of you." Could it actually *be* him? Had the rattlesticks got to him at the church? Nona moaned in horror. It was her worst nightmare come true.

A firm hand pressed down on Nona's shoulder. She jumped with fright before she saw it was Serafin. Serafin held her gaze and, as if she'd read Nona's mind, said, "Nona. It *isn't* him."

Nona couldn't speak, but she nodded. This was what Serafin had warned her about. She found she could breathe once more.

The voice of Uncle Antoni came again, its tone harder this time. "We were supposed to stick together," it said. "Nona, why did you leave?" Her breath froze again in her body. She *knew* it wasn't Uncle Antoni saying those things, but the words needled her like icicles.

"It's reading you," said Serafin, "but it's just a mockery of your uncle. A twisted mirror to your worst fears."

Serafin's words seemed distant. Nona trusted her. But what if she was wrong?

"Castor?" came another voice. It was a man's, one Nona didn't recognize. "Look at you," the voice said in disgust. "You've become the monster you always were."

Castor shrieked and took off from Nona's shoulder, wheeling above the rattlesticks' heads. He had a crystal bottle of the lake water in his claws which he poured on them from above. Those it touched hissed and crumpled into piles of sticks, including the one who'd imitated the man – and Uncle Antoni.

They *were* only imitations, she knew that. A dose of anger entered the churn of her emotions. How dare they toy with them like that?

Castor must have felt it too. He dived through the wall of mist and disappeared.

"Castor," Nona called. "Come back!"

"Let him go," said Serafin. "He can handle himself."

Adrenalin surged through Nona. She didn't want to stand there any more. She wanted to stop these terrible creatures. She took a step forwards, but Serafin held her back.

"Wait until they come to us," she said, "or you may stumble into the bog yourself. They *will* come. When they do, I'll fend them off. If any get past me, touch your staff to their chests. The lake water will make them crumble."

Mist began to collect around more of the rattlestick skulls, forming the ghostly impression of faces. Some were muttering and Nona realized why: they were spells, to change their faces. No doubt using scraps of stolen magic... She couldn't bear to think what would happen if this army – and the Soldier – got their hands on all the power they wanted. It really did feel as if the rattlesticks could see inside each of them, and mirror their worst fears – just as Serafin had said. These were far worse – and far more dangerous – than the scouts she'd previously encountered.

"Serafin? Is that you?" one of them said. It was at the front of a large group of seven or more and getting closer than ever. "You and Alesea should never have meddled in human affairs, Serafin. You're not like us any more. We don't want either of you back after what you've created."

After what you've created? Did it mean the Soldier? But Nona didn't have long to wonder, because Serafin was lunging forwards and thrusting her staff into the rattlestick's ribs. It made a hissing sound, like a snake, or steam, and fell away – just a pile of twigs on the ground.

Nona wondered how many times Serafin had heard the rattlesticks say similar things to try to hurt her. Even knowing that they weren't real, it had to be unbearable.

But if it was, Serafin didn't show it. She stood in front of Nona now, swishing and stabbing with her staff. More and more rattlesticks crumbled, their bodies scattered across the floor, or billowed away with the mist, like ash. Nona clutched her stick until her hands ached.

Two rattlesticks managed to slip past Serafin while she was occupied with three others, and came closer. Nona didn't waste any time before plunging her stick into the first one's chest. It hissed and disintegrated in front of her eyes. Feeling more confident, Nona wheeled round and destroyed the second rattlestick. A feeling of something between excitement and fear jangled in her veins.

Another rattlestick was coming now, and this one was fast. It called her name. "Nona."

Nona recognized the voice immediately. But it didn't make the shock any more bearable when she saw the ghost of her mother's face. "You've forgotten us, haven't you?" said her mother. "You and your uncle have got your own neat little family without us now. And after all I did for you." She reached out to touch Nona. Nona backed away, but she held onto her staff tight. She ought to touch the rattlestick's chest, she knew. But something stopped her. It was the look in her mother's eyes. The disappointment. How she'd longed to see her mother's face again – but not like this. Nona's legs trembled.

"I would never have forgotten *you*," said Nona's mother. There was no mistaking the accusation. The venom of it. Nona couldn't bear it. She squeezed her eyes shut and thrust out the staff. There was a hiss, and a pattering sound, as if someone had scattered a handful of soil. And when she opened them her mother had gone.

Nona was alone with the thundering of blood through her body, the tirade of thoughts flashing through her mind, and the shaking of her own bones.

One of the rattlesticks whispered some words and at that moment the direction of the wind changed. It carried the mist with it. A spell – it had to be. The mist crept closer until it was all around Nona. Castor and Serafin were nowhere to be seen, though she could hear them battling further in. Nona didn't have any time to find them. Perhaps Serafin could have countered the rattlestick's spell, driven the mist back, but without her Nona couldn't do a thing. Another rattlestick came out of the mist, running this time.

It was her brother.

Nona leaped back, startled, and braced the stick in her hands. After her mother she didn't plan to hesitate this time. She gritted her teeth. "I know you aren't who you pretend to be," she shouted, as much to convince herself as anything. "You're not my brother. I don't care what you say." The rattlestick didn't speak. It only advanced – tall, confident, silent.

Nona screamed – and attacked. But there was no hiss of steam this time. The realization hit her at once: the lake water... It had worn off. The rattlestick wearing her brother's face faltered, but kept coming closer. She hit out again and again, but in her fright her aim wasn't very good. Its arm came away, and then part of its chest.

Still, he didn't say a word. He didn't have to. All it would take was one touch – and Nona would be like him... She would become a rattlestick. And her life force would go straight to the Soldier.

Nona turned and fled, fumbling with the latch of her bag as she did so. She plunged her hand in and pulled out the first thing she found: a pouch of the dried herbs. She couldn't outrun the rattlestick. It was coming too fast. Her brother had always been the only one who could beat her at tag. If she could create a patch of mist, using the herbs, perhaps she could hide from it. Confuse it. Then strike. She had to think of the rattlestick as it, or she feared she would start to believe it was her brother... Nona had her fingers ready to fling the herbs into the air when she heard him creak by her ear. She flung the half-opened pouch over her shoulder.

The rattlestick made a noise of surprise: it had hit him in the face. Hopefully, some of the escaped herbs had gone in his eyes too. Perhaps this would stop it from seeing her and she could get away. Nona made a dart up the hill for Serafin's home. But something grabbed her arm.

The rattlestick.

20

NONA FELL FORWARDS. THE STICK CLATTERED OUT of her hand and rolled away from her. She twisted to find the rattlestick sprawled across the ground amid a low mist which must have been all her bag of herbs had mustered, and one pale, skeletal hand clamped firmly around her upper arm. The rattlestick with her brother's face said, "Tag."

That was it. Already she could feel the cold spreading out from his touch – through her flesh and along her arm, turning her bones brittle. She was becoming one of them. Nona cried out and hit the rattlestick with all her might. It crumpled against her attack and, with a final hard whack, disintegrated into a mound of loose parts. They rattled and rolled across the ground before coming to rest in a sprawl of debris.

"*Craaw!* Over here – she's over here." Castor dived through the archway, followed by Serafin, wide-eyed as she hurried up the path. Castor cleared the distance between them in seconds. His landing on her shoulder was so heavy it knocked Nona back.

"Watch it," she said, but she was woozy. Her head ached, and grey had started to cloud the corners of her vision. Her neck, when she turned it, creaked…

"*Craaw!*" shouted Castor in her ear, flapping and nudging. "*Craaw. Craaw. Craaw!*"

Through a haze, Nona watched Serafin stride towards her.

"Don't move," she commanded, crouching by Nona's arm. What was Serafin going to do? Nona was becoming a rattlestick. Her entire arm had turned numb. Soon that numbness would envelop her body. Her senses. Her mind.

Would the touch of Serafin's staff kill her? Is that what she was going to do? Put Nona out of her misery?

No. She wasn't ready. "Stop!" she called. She struggled with all her might, but Serafin was strong. She clamped hold of Nona's arm at the elbow.

More softly this time, but with no less authority, she said, "I told you not to move." She lay down her staff and held her palm against Nona's arm. Perhaps it was a product of her imagination, but through her greying vision the lightning scar like the tendrils of a fern on Serafin's arm seemed to shine.

Nona's arm hissed – just as the rattlesticks' bodies did before they'd crumbled. And it felt like a thousand needles piercing her skin.

When Nona opened her eyes it was daylight, and the rafters of Serafin's roof were above her. She'd been aware of the rhythm of the mill wheel as she rose up from sleep, and the sound of it gently turning filled her with calm. Her eyes still closed, her sleepy fingers sought out the half-heart beneath her pillow for comfort. It was strange how she always found it, wherever it was. As if the half-heart was just another part of her.

A voice near her ear said, "Wake up, Nona. You've been dreaming." It was her mother's voice, and it seemed like the most natural thing in the world that she should be there. Nona breathed a deep, satisfied sigh. *Just a little bit longer.*

"Nona? Nona! Look, Serafin, I think she's waking up." That wasn't her mother, but a boy. And not her brother. Someone else...

Castor.

Everything came back to her in a rush. The rattlesticks. Their battle. Her arm. Nona sat upright in the bed. Her head swam, and she was forced to lean back again. Relief flooded her body. She was alive – even though the rattlestick had touched her. How?

Castor squatted at the foot of her bed. "So," he said with a relieved grin. "How's the war wound?" Despite the joke, he studied Nona carefully as he clambered across the blanket to sit next to her elbow, swishing his imp tail. "You've slept all morning and through teatime, lazybones," he added with a grin.

Nona ignored his question. "What happened?" she asked instead. Her mouth felt dry, which made swallowing – and speaking – hard. But now that she was less dizzy she could sit up. Only a bluish shadow – bruise-like – on her skin showed any sign that anything had happened to it.

"What do you remember?"

Nona thought. "My brother – a *rattlestick*, I mean, grabbed my arm. And then you and Serafin came back for me. And—"

"Then I healed you."

Serafin moved out of the shadows by the door and took a seat beside Nona's bed. She nudged Castor – gently but firmly – out of the way.

"Thank you. H-how did you—" Nona began. Serafin waved her patterned arm and cut Nona short. "That's for me to know. But you were very lucky I was there." Nona let out her breath. It didn't bear thinking about what a close call it had been. A feeling of intense coldness began to crystallize inside Nona's chest. She had faced a handful of rattlesticks – and lost. If it hadn't been for Serafin's help, and Castor's, she would have become one of them, while the Soldier would have what he wanted: her life energy. And the rattlesticks were apparently nothing compared to the Soldier. "I... I let you down," said Nona. "I'm sorry."

"No." Serafin placed her hand over the tender skin on Nona's arm where the rattlestick had touched. "You listened and you learned, and you showed great courage. No one could have predicted how many there would be. I'm proud of you, Nona." Serafin's eyes sparkled, and she looked away. "It's me who should be sorry. For putting you at risk. I was angry with Alesea for doing that, and now I've done the same."

"It's all right," said Nona. She searched for the right thing to say, and the energy to say it. "I'm glad you showed me how to fight them." It had been a terrible ordeal. But she'd done it. They all had. No one could take that away from her. And next time, perhaps she'd do better. For all the terror she'd felt last night, the confrontation had ignited something in her: a tiny spark of courage.

Serafin smiled. "All the people you saw," she said softly. "Everything they said…"

Nona's throat tightened at Serafin's words and she found herself clenching the blanket in her fist. Her mother's misty face flashed before her eyes – and her brother's. Their words echoed in her mind. She knew the rattlesticks had only been trying to hurt her. But what they'd said was true. She had found a new kind of family – and peace – with Uncle Antoni. And although she thought of her mother and brother all the time, what if she had dishonoured their memory in some way by moving on?

Serafin must have understood the expression on Nona's face, because she said, "They read your fears, Nona. Ones so deep that even you may not be aware of them. And they reflect them back at you – like a mirror that shows only bad things. They can do it because they are held together by the same thing as fear. But it doesn't matter how solid they seem." She rested her hand on Nona's arm, and squeezed. "The rattlesticks are just detritus – and their words are nothing but air."

They were quiet then, listening to the steady clunk and turn of the mill wheel. Eventually, Serafin stood up. "Get yourself washed and ready, eat and take some time to recover," Serafin said. "I must speak with Alesea about how best to keep you safe after this. The Soldier will know now that I'm harbouring a child here, and that you could be the one he needs. And I must prepare for tonight's battle. My supplies are dangerously low."

Guilt struck Nona hard. That was partly because of her being there. Serafin's gaze flickered across Nona, before she lowered her head, and stalked out of the room.

When she was washed, dressed and ready, her glass fragment safely in her pocket alongside the pocketstone, Nona pushed open the door to Serafin's workroom. Serafin sat at the table, pulling leaves off the same plant as yesterday. Castor wasn't there.

Nona took a seat and began to pluck off the leaves too. She didn't have to look up to know that Serafin had paused in her work and was watching Nona with interest. Nona could feel it spilling out of her like sunlight.

"I'd like to ask you something," said Nona. Still she didn't look up into Serafin's eyes.

There was a long pause before Serafin said, "Go on."

"You're battling those rattlesticks every night, and you're doing it on your own. Why doesn't Alesea help? You're supposed to be spirit-sisters, aren't you? It's not right!"

"Help?" Serafin scoffed. "I don't need help." The silence drew out between them – and Nona let it. Both of them knew that wasn't true. But would Serafin admit it? Nona shifted in her seat. When Serafin spoke again, her voice was quieter.

"The truth is, Alesea and I must stay apart, in order to spread the Soldier's forces more thinly. If Alesea came here we would face double the number of rattlesticks, and the Soldier would be able to concentrate his full power against us. Besides, Alesea's magic doesn't work in the same way as mine. She is better at stealth, which is why she is the one readying the umbrafell." Serafin sighed and shook her head. "Sadly, there's no choice, Nona. As much as I miss her, we must face our burdens alone. However impossible they may be."

Nona couldn't help but stare up at Serafin now. "But … does she know what you're up against?" The look on Serafin's face suggested not. Nona wanted to tell Serafin that it was all right to ask for help. Though she knew from experience how hard that could be. How impossible, when you felt that the weight of a burden was yours alone. Especially if you feared your pleas might be rejected. Nona loved Uncle Antoni, but any time she'd tried to talk about her mother and brother – or what had happened to them – he stopped her. And as much as she hated to admit it, that hurt.

"I—" Serafin gave Nona a half-smile that, for all Serafin's steel, looked almost embarrassed. Then her expression became sad and she looked away. "Did you know," she said, "that a hare will hide while the entire field burns, and only think to run when the flames are almost upon it? *I'm* supposed to be the strong one."

"Serafin," Nona said. "Why don't you just give her a chance to help? She should at least know you're struggling."

Serafin pursed her lips at the word *struggling*, but didn't correct Nona. Instead she said, "On the day the Soldier gained his power – the moment he put one foot in our world – it was because he saw Alesea. Alesea, with all her cunning and stealth. She has never quite forgiven herself for dropping her guard, or for what he's become. For being seen. It's made her withdraw even more."

Nona gasped. Serafin was describing the moment

she'd witnessed, with the help of the half-heart: the young officer who'd glanced into the glass and seen Alesea's reflection, she was sure of it. But there was something she didn't understand. "Why did it matter so much, Alesea being seen by him?" Nona asked. "I've seen you both loads."

Serafin leaned back. "It's the *when* that's important," she said. "He glimpsed Alesea at the moment of his death. A sniper had been lying in wait, you see. But the Soldier called out to Alesea and, in the instant he would have died, unwittingly stepped into our world. He changed his fate, becoming part spirit. The sniper's shot missed. He lived," Serafin raised her eyebrows. "And was touched by magic.

"We hid the Soldier's memories from him as best as we could," Serafin went on. "To conceal his power from him. It was better that way, since we didn't know how a human might cope with the burden. The war ended and we kept an eye on his progress. He married and had a child but he *felt* different from other humans – as if he didn't fit in any more. We saw it all. His withdrawal from them. He had dreams – visions. Prophetic ones." Serafin fixed her gaze on Nona. Nona's mind reeled. Prophetic visions – like the ones she had when she held the half-heart? But Serafin continued. "He soon rediscovered his magic, of course. And us. Then his son died, and neither of us could save him. The Soldier felt betrayed – outraged. He believed we could have done something more – that we should have. His bitterness grew, as did his obsession with bringing his child back from the otherworld. He created his glass heart, to steal our power – and to try to reverse death itself."

Serafin began plucking the leaves again. She sighed. "Perhaps our kin were right when they told us we should have never meddled in human affairs. But war is so brutal. Alesea and I wanted to help. Now, while the Soldier gets more powerful, we are merely fighting his fires. Even his rattlesticks threaten to overrun us."

Nona shuddered. All of a sudden she felt cold. She had so many questions but no idea where to start.

"Do not lose hope, brave Nona," said Serafin with a smile. "Things are different now. You are the key to defeating the Soldier for good. You and your own magic. We may be united yet." At this Nona couldn't help smiling. She hoped so. She hoped they could beat the Soldier – together. And yet she still wondered: *why her*? And how could they be so sure she was the one the Soldier needed? The feeling sat uncomfortably inside her, like something hard and unyielding, that she still didn't know the whole truth.

"Now," said Serafin. "Although I am grateful for your help, the fact remains you ought to be resting. I have been in touch with Alesea and she will come soon to plan our next steps. When she does I ... I will be truthful with her about what I face." She glanced at her empty bucket. "Then I will need to go to the forbidden lake before midnight," she murmured to herself. Her expression was fretful again, the shadows beneath her eyes showing. "We used the very last of my supplies in our battle last night."

Nona felt a stab of guilt. Their low supplies were because of her. As if Serafin didn't have enough problems.

21

To distract herself from her thoughts, Nona took herself outside and pulled out her sketchbook, intending to draw some of the plants. Everything looked as though it had been dipped in ice – leaves, blossoms, red and white toadstools – encrusted with frost-like jewel clusters. Even Nona's breath turned to mist, but that only reminded her of the rattlesticks and the way they had worn other people's faces. Nona pulled her hands up inside the sleeves of her brother's old jumper and hugged herself for warmth.

Ever since the battle with the rattlesticks, she had felt emotionally delicate. As though she were made of glass. *Draw*, Uncle Antoni would say. She flicked to a clean page in her sketchbook.

Nona found herself thinking how the scene in front of her would make a wonderful stained-glass window. It looked icy and magical, but with signs of spring starting to cut through. Her mind fizzed with ideas for how she could capture it in glass, before her excitement turned to worry. Had it been selfish to leave Uncle Antoni alone? Shouldn't she be there, looking after him while he was vulnerable?

"I'm sorry I can't help you more, Castor," came Serafin's voice from somewhere in the garden. Nona froze, her pencil hovering above the page. She didn't mean to listen in on a private conversation, but she was intrigued. "The magic she used to tie you to this physical form is near-impossible to unpick. Alesea should never have attempted this kind of magic. It's not her speciality – it's mine."

"That's true," came Castor's voice, quiet. "But you weren't there."

Silence followed.

Finally, Serafin spoke again. "You're right. But I've been doing all I can to help ever since. Try this new blend of the tincture tonight. Though, if it doesn't work…"

"…There's nothing else you can do. We've tried everything else. Thanks anyway, Serafin."

Serafin sighed. "I will keep thinking, Castor. About your predicament."

The voices grew closer, as though they were walking together through the gardens from the mill house. Soon they would appear close by, and it would be clear that Nona had been listening. Nona gathered up her things and backed away along the path.

The gardens and nearby woodland were so peaceful that it was hard to believe this had been the scene of last night's battle. When Nona came to the spot where she'd fallen, where the rattlestick had grabbed her, she couldn't stop herself from shivering.

A rustle came from the nearby trees. Nona froze. More rattlesticks? Her heart pounded. She knew they could only come out at night or in shadowy places. It was afternoon, but the trees did cast shadows...

"Come out," she said at once. "Show yourself." She refused to run. She reached for her stick which she'd slipped through the straps of her rucksack – in an imitation of how Serafin carried hers.

The tree rustled again, and creaked.

Then Alesea emerged from the shadows. The hood on her fur cape was pulled up around her face. On such an icy day it looked snug. "Hello, darling Nona," she said with her usual bewitching smile.

Nona let out the breath she'd been holding. "Uncle Antoni," she said. "Is he all right?"

Alesea looked at her, as if puzzled that he would be her first thought. "Yes," she said with a wave of her hand. "As far as I know, he's well."

"As far as you know?" Nona's voice rose in panic. "Aren't you looking out for him? It's because of your spell that he's defenceless in the first place."

This time Alesea's smile vanished like smoke and her expression became one of worry. "Caring too much about what happens to other people will only hurt you, Nona," she said, moving past her. "It can put you in danger." Alesea paused, before adding, "Besides, all this magic in front of you, at your fingertips, and that's what you concern yourself with?"

Nona resented Alesea for what she'd said, but the talk of magic intrigued her. Ever since she'd taken flight in her second skin she'd had a burning curiosity to know more. To learn her own magic. To fly again.

"How do you do it, anyway?" Nona mumbled. "Move through trees and stones, I mean?" Her cheeks flushed when Alesea looked back at her. The spirit looked smug.

"Oh, it's simple," Alesea smiled. "When you know how." She drew closer. Nona could tell she'd sparked Alesea's excitement with her question. "It's about how you see them," she said, wrapping an arm around Nona's shoulder and guiding her to the tree. "They aren't dead ends, but gateways. Tunnels, if you like. For a human it's all about imagination, I expect. You imagine yourself into the tree, or stone." Alesea lifted Nona's arm, placing it against the tree. Ice melted against her fingers, behind which Nona could feel the comforting warmth of a living thing. Her palm tingled. What would happen next?

"If it helps," said Alesea in Nona's ear, "say these words: *Let me through to the hidden path.*"

Alesea's whisper lingered in the air, hung around them like mist. The sound of rushing wind began to build in Nona's ears. Her fingers pushed through the tree, melting into it, as if it wasn't even there.

"That's it," said Alesea, and gently drew Nona's hand back from the tree. The rushing sound stopped. All that was left was the sound of Nona's quick, excited breathing.

"Congratulations," said Alesea. "Not even the Soldier can do that." She beamed and walked away. Her words gave Nona's heart a little leap of pride – and hope that she and the Soldier might not be so mismatched in strength after all. But Alesea's sudden absence made Nona feel cold.

Nona watched her walk down the path towards the mill house, where Serafin and Castor now stood. When Serafin and Alesea saw each other, they hugged tight.

Alesea cupped Castor's imp-face in her hands, and petted him.

Castor spotted Nona further along the path and ran to her, while Serafin and Alesea retreated inside. Was it Nona's imagination or did he look different today? More human? It was something about his face, which looked reordered somehow. His nose was longer and his forehead broader. Although he still had scales, and a tail.

As Castor approached, Nona noticed he carried a small red pouch in one thick-fingered hand. Perhaps inside it was the tincture he and Serafin had been discussing – whatever that was for.

"How're you feeling?" asked Castor, clambering up Nona's leg in a clumsy attempt to get to her shoulder.

"Hey. Careful!"

"You know, you gave us a real scare last night," he said, finally reaching his perch. "Let's not do that ever, ever, ever, ever…"

"Castor."

"…ever, ever, *ever* again."

"Castor, come on. Let's go."

"Well, I'm supposed to make sure you stay here, but all right," he said. He sounded very chirpy. Chirpier, at least, than Nona would have expected after what she'd heard of his conversation with Serafin. And Nona still couldn't get over how different his face looked. "Where are we going?"

Nona's gaze was fixed on the mill house, where Serafin and Alesea would now be sitting inside. What Alesea had said – that caring about other people was dangerous – made her bristle every time she thought of it.

Nona didn't need lecturing on the pain of caring for people who were gone. But she refused to let it stop her from helping the people who weren't. And to start with she was going to help Serafin.

"Hey. Wakey, wakey," said Castor, patting her lightly on the cheek. "Where are we going?" he asked.

Nona clenched her jaw. "We're going to the lake," she said. Serafin had enough on her plate already. Fetching the water for her was only right. Even if it would be dangerous.

22

"THE FORBIDDEN LAKE?" SHRIEKED CASTOR IN Nona's ear. "The *forbidden* one?"

"That's the one I had in mind," said Nona. "Want to help me look for it?" She had already started walking. She marched under the archway and started on the path that led past the bog the rattlesticks had risen from last night. She hated to think how many would crawl out of it again, come dark. Even in the daytime the sight of it sent a shiver through her.

"No. Anyway, I'm supposed to make sure you stay *here*." Castor clambered around her head and onto her other shoulder, clonking her on the nose with the bag he still had wrapped around his fingers.

"Ouch. Stop it!"

"We don't want to go to that lake," said Castor in her ear. His breath was warm and wet and irritating.

She gave him a nudge to shift him round onto the other shoulder.

"*You* don't," said Nona. "*I* do. Serafin used the last of her supplies against the rattlesticks and she needs more. I'm going to get some for her. She saved my life, Castor. It's the least I can do."

But Castor still wasn't convinced. He rippled yellow and white with apparent fear. Although, Nona noticed, he hadn't stopped her – nor had he left her to go alone. "All right, listen. That lake is…" Castor shuddered violently. "It's a bad place. It's an umbrafell like the church, which makes it magical – and *really* powerful. But its power comes at a price. Just touching a drop of it, or even looking at your own reflection, can give people visions."

"So what?" chipped in Nona. "My glass gives me visions too." Nona felt Castor tense. He gave another shudder.

"Not like this, you haven't. Spirits have seen prophecies of doom," he said, counting on his bulbous fingers. "Humans have foreseen their own deaths. And you've seen what it does to the rattlesticks. Leave it to Serafin, Nona. Nothing good will come of us going there. Nothing. *Noo-thing.*"

Nona didn't reply. She remembered well Serafin's warnings at the mill house not to touch the water or go anywhere near it. She'd be lying if she said those warnings didn't scare her. And what about the Soldier himself? He was still out there. She touched the pocketstone. At least this would hide her from him... Although it had only been intended to get her to Serafin's house. Alesea had said it would last for no more than a day or two. Its magic would surely wear off soon. Was it her imagination, or did its surface feel chalkier than usual?

But after everything Serafin had done for them, Nona desperately wanted to do this for her. And there was a part of her that wanted to prove herself. "We just won't look into it," Nona said eventually. "We'll scoop up some water in my flask and carry it straight back to Serafin before they even know we've been anywhere. I'll even close my eyes when I do it if that makes you feel better, Castor."

Castor let out a deep, frustrated sigh. "It doesn't!" he said, although he still didn't leave her to go alone, she noted. "But how do you propose we find it? Oh, don't tell me. You've got your glass, haven't you?"

Nona nodded. She pulled the glass fragment – her half-heart – out of her pocket, and grinned. "I know we're close," she said. "Serafin said as much. And I reckon I can make it work this time."

Castor didn't reply. A flutter and a shift in weight told Nona that he'd gone back to his crow form, and if there was one thing she knew full well it was that she'd get no more out of him.

❧≫≫≫➤

This part of the woods was laced through and through with weaving spirit paths, their warm pinpricks of light glowing like lines of shining insects all around. Nona could hardly move for them. She stared through the pink hue of her glass fragment, looking for glimpses of the recent past – and soon found Serafin's image crossing a path to and fro with her bucket.

Maybe it was fear, but Castor was particularly fidgety, folding and unfolding his wings for no reason. Preening. Clawing at her shoulder. Although she could tell it wasn't on purpose – merely that he wasn't paying attention. He was agitated, she knew that much. The string of the little red bag was wrapped around one of his clawed feet, and the bag itself – that must have contained Serafin's tincture – dangled against her shoulder. What did he need it for? But Nona didn't ask. She shouldn't have listened in in the first place.

She trudged on. Trees blocked out the sky, and it was much darker and colder here than in Serafin's garden. Rattlesticks could be a real possibility – so Nona stayed on guard.

Even though she'd wanted to come, she glanced behind her, yearning for the warmth and comfort of her new friend. Through a rare clearing in the trees she noticed that the sky had turned an eerie blue-grey and the moon was visible, despite night still being a way off. The moon was full and round and bright white against the murky sky. Nona chewed her lip. Had she set off later from Serafin's than she thought? After sleeping past midday she hadn't managed to get a grip on the time at all.

But the next second Castor drew her attention. He scratched and squawked as though in terrible pain. Then he fell from Nona's shoulder like a stone.

"Castor? Castor!" Nona fell to her knees beside his small body. With his wings folded, his claws tucked up into his body and his head turned to the side with closed eyes, he looked as though he had died. She touched his wing gently. "Wake up. Please."

He felt warm to the touch, but that didn't offer much comfort. If he had died suddenly, his blood wouldn't have had time to cool. Had his heart stopped? She'd heard that could happen to birds and other small creatures who'd had a shock, and he'd seemed panicked.

Nona glanced around but saw nothing that might have frightened him. She shook him gently. "Come on, Castor. You're scaring me." Still he didn't move.

An icy wind wove through the trees and whipped Nona's face. It ruffled the downy black feathers on Castor's soft, upturned tummy. Slowly, beneath the light from the moon, something began to happen to the tiny body. It began to grow. Nona pulled her hand back, quick as a reflex. She leaped up, backed away. Castor's body continued to change, growing out of its shape and into a new one. Until it had two sets of legs and arms, sticking out of a dark woollen duffle coat. And a beakless face beneath a mass of long, dark hair.

The shape of a human boy.

Castor – or rather the boy that Nona now stared at – rubbed his face and groaned. Then he sat bolt upright. Nona jumped. Straight away, he felt around in the moss at his sides.

"Wha— How?" Nona began. She shook herself and tried again. "Castor? Is that you?" But she knew it had to be. He even had the string of the small red pouch tangled around his bare toes. Her breath quickened, raising a little fog in the cold, dense air. This was incredible.

Castor searched around in the undergrowth for

something until he finally found the tiny red bag he'd carried with him. He reached down and scrabbled to untangle the cord from his toes. He undid the bag clumsily, as if unused to the size of his fingers, and pulled one of Serafin's tiny crystal bottles out of it. The draught inside was opaline, like bottled moonlight, or semi-translucent milk-glass.

"What's it for?" Nona gasped, awe-struck.

Castor looked at her for the first time in his human form. His eyes were wide, his pupils large and round and dark. Nona had gazed into them before: in his imp form. While everything else had changed, his eyes were just the same. He had freckles on his nose. He must have been about eleven, like her.

"It's to break Alesea's spell." His voice came out croaky, as if his vocal cords were still catching up. "So I don't have to be a *thing* any more."

"Alesea did that to you?" Nona stared. "And – you're really a boy? Not a crow. Or a…" She still didn't know what to call his other self – that strange, scaled amalgamation of creatures with the devil-like tail. "Hey, you could've told me!" Now she felt indignant.

"I *was* a boy. Once." Castor looked at the milky liquid inside its crystal container. "Now I'm only ever human during the full moon. Since Alesea put her spell on me, that is."

"Castor, that's horrible," said Nona, "but I don't understand. Why do you still do as she asks, even after she cursed you like this?"

"It wasn't meant to be a curse," he said. His eyes shone. "My parents and I were inside the church the night it was bombed. We thought we'd be safe there, and so did everyone else. No planes ever came this far over from Portsmouth before." Castor scratched the ground with his finger, like he would usually claw at it as a crow. "But we weren't. Everyone was killed. I lived because Alesea found me still breathing – just. She saved my life, but to fix my injuries more easily she gave me my second skin – of a crow. The power to transform the way that she does.

"But healing isn't her normal magic and I wasn't ready for my second skin and something didn't work when I came to change back," he went on. "It means the closest I can get to a human form is…" He shrugged and stared deeply into the shimmering contents of the bottle. "Well, you've seen it. No matter how hard I try, I can't become fully human again. Not unless it's a full moon, when Alesea's power is strongest." He jerked his head at the sky. "Then for one night I turn back, whether I want to or not. If I drink this, though…"

"…You might be able to change back," finished Nona. "For ever." Nona released his arm. So Alesea had *saved* Castor. Or at least tried to. No wonder Castor was loyal to her, no matter what she did. And she'd taken him in when his parents died, just as Uncle Antoni had done for her. She was all he had. Maybe she even felt like a mother to him. She remembered how Alesea had stroked his face and petted him in the garden. There'd been tenderness there.

Castor smiled weakly. "It's funny, my ma and pa were always calling me names. *Castor, you little beast! I didn't raise a monster. Get in that cellar and stay there, this time. Castor, you imp. What have you done to my washing? You wait 'til your father hears. He'll give you a hiding you won't forget.*" He chuckled mirthlessly.

Nona's heart sank. She couldn't find the words through her anger and sadness for Castor. Instead she asked, "Did they punish you a lot?"

He shrugged. "I suppose, but I was always misbehaving. Maybe my new form is punishment for it." Nona didn't believe that. He was only a boy, and to be called such horrible names, and beaten... She knew some parents believed in strict discipline and hitting was quite common, but the thought of what Castor must have been through made her feel sick. He didn't deserve it then, or now.

"At least they cared, I suppose, in their way," he

said. "Alesea's just happy as long as I run her errands…"
Before Nona could answer, Castor threw his head back
and drank Serafin's draught. He shuddered and wiped
his mouth with his woollen sleeve.

Nona watched him closely for a few seconds,
studying him. She wasn't sure what she was expecting
to happen. Fireworks? "When will we know if it's
worked?" she asked.

"At the dawn of the next day," said Castor. "When
that happens I'll either stay like this, or I'll turn back
into a crow. All I know is it tasted disgusting enough
that it *could* work." He gave Nona a cheeky grin and
pushed himself up off the ground. "Come on," he
said. "Let's go and find this forbidden lake you're so
desperate to take us to."

Nona held up the glass to the spirit path again,
and she saw Serafin's past self heading towards what
looked like a clearing beyond the trees.

And, as soon as they arrived in the clearing, Nona
knew this was the place.

All noise – the rustle of leaves, the sounds of birds
and small creatures – stopped. The only thing they
could hear was the water of the lake as it lapped
against the black, rotting bank.

Everything about this place felt wrong.

Castor grabbed Nona's arm urgently. "Keep an

eye out for rattlesticks," he warned. The shadows fell thicker around here.

When Nona reached the water's edge, her first instinct was to look down. She stopped herself just in time, remembering Serafin's warnings. She chewed the inside of her cheek, wondering how best to get the water. Would she really be able to avoid looking? The idea of glimpsing something terrible filled her with dread. What if she saw the Soldier? Might she see him taking her life for his son's?

Iciness radiated from the surface of the water and she guessed from its coolness that it had a depth she couldn't begin to fathom. Bottomless, Serafin had called it, although Nona didn't know how that could be true.

Nona kneeled, took off her rucksack and unbuttoned it. Instead of glancing into the water she kept her gaze fixed on Castor beside her, who looked back with worried eyes. She let her eyes wander a little – taking in the bruised sky, the wide expanse of dark, lapping water beneath it. Mist hung around in patches and odd dark lumps rose out of the water around the edges – large rotten logs and crumbling rocks.

And on the far side of the water was a man.

Nona held her breath. Wisps of mist passed around him. Like her, he was kneeling, but his gaze was locked on the lake: he hadn't spotted Nona or Castor.

"Castor." She nudged him. "Look."

"What is it?"

"Over there."

Castor looked. "There's nothing."

"There is," Nona whispered. "A man on the opposite bank. You'll see him in a minute." Though when the mist cleared there was only a jagged piece of stone where the man had been. Nona let out a sigh of relief. It must have just looked like someone sitting there. Perhaps it was the odd, creepy light in this clearing.

Nona pulled her flask out of her rucksack, then tipped the contents away and shuffled as close as she could get to the edge of the lake. She squinted until she was peering out through the shadows of her eyelashes. *Please don't see anything*, she repeated in her head. *Please don't see anything.*

"Here," Castor said. He held onto her arm so she could lean further out – over the water. Just as she was about to scoop up the water, Castor yanked her back.

"Ow! What—" Nona began. But Castor was frozen, his sights fixed on something across the lake.

This time there was no mistaking it. There really was a man – and no rock to be found at all. He was kneeling at the very edge of the lake where the grass bank formed an overhang. He was stock still, his body bent over the water. And he was dressed like a soldier.

23

THE SIGHT OF THE MAN'S ARMY UNIFORM MADE Nona's stomach flip over. He was a soldier. Perhaps *the* Soldier.

"Time to go," said Castor. "Now." He was still holding on tight to Nona. "It could be one of the Soldier's tricks," he hissed.

Terror coursed through Nona, from her head to her feet. She could easily have let Castor pull her away from that place. But then… Something in her told her that this wasn't the Soldier. He looked too human, for one thing. The way he hunched over the water in that urgent, crooked pose. The fearful expression.

"No," said Nona. "I don't think he's dangerous." She eyed the man again. He cut a tragic figure, unmoving against the sky. "He might need our help."

Before Castor could beg her not to, Nona skirted

the bank towards the man on the other side. Whatever was wrong with this man, she was sure that Castor would want no part of it. So she was surprised when his fingers found her hand. They were as cool and slightly damp as when he was an imp.

The man didn't look up, even when they were only a few paces away. He had a prominent forehead, thick, dark eyebrows and a strong nose. He was handsome and stocky. But the expression on his face gave Nona goosebumps. He seemed frozen with horror.

Nona cleared her throat. The man didn't lift his gaze from the water. "Excuse me." This time she did catch his attention.

"Be quiet," he said in a hushed voice. "I'm trying to hear them."

He hadn't even looked up – as if knowing who she was didn't matter to him at all. Only whatever he saw in the water. Though the only way to discover what, exactly, was to look herself... If she looked at an angle, perhaps she could avoid looking directly or seeing her own reflection? Nona felt light-headed with fear, but something in her needed to know what held this man so enthralled.

With a glance at Castor, Nona edged closer to the man. When she was right beside him, she leaned over the bank as far as she dared. Castor cried out in protest when he realized what she was doing. But Nona held her nerve. If she did it right, she wouldn't see her own reflection – only his.

If she did it right.

At first, all Nona could see were flashes of light bouncing off the lake's surface. Then something shifted and she saw the man's reflection staring back at him. He was surrounded by other men. All of them soldiers. All of the same regiment, it looked like. Their mouths were moving, as if they were speaking, each of them at once, though not a single sound came from their lips.

Now that Nona really studied the man's reflection, it didn't have the licks of grey in the eyebrows and hair, or the crow's feet around the eyes that she could see in the man next to her.

"My name is Will," said the man. "These are my friends. Or … they were." He raised an arm slowly, as if moving took a great deal of effort, and pointed each one out in turn.

"Danby. Taverner. Khan. Smith. All of them were killed in the war."

Nona couldn't understand it. None of it made sense, and Will looked preoccupied again. "What does it mean, Castor?" But Castor only shrugged.

Nona noticed with a start that where Will's body rested against the ground, his legs curled under him, and the folds of his clothes and angle of his legs looked more solid. More like ... stone. As if they'd been set – sunken – into the ground.

Nona took a step back. This wasn't right. There was definitely magic at play. When she thought she saw a rock earlier, perhaps her eyes hadn't been tricking her after all. It looked as though Will was becoming part of the landscape.

"Will?" said Nona slowly. "Exactly how long have you been sitting next to this enchanted lake?"

A light rain had started. It hung in the air and left jewels of moisture clinging to their hair and clothes. Nona could see that much of Will's body – his khaki uniform – had turned to quartz-flecked rock now, and it was climbing up his neck. It wouldn't be long before it enveloped him completely.

"I've lost track," said Will simply. "I try and try to hear them, but I can't. I think they're telling me that I should be with them. That I should be..." The faces of his fallen friends gazed out of the water, their mouths still moving soundlessly. And, at the centre, Will himself was doing the same. "I don't think I could move from this place now," he added, his voice a mere whisper catching in his throat. "Even if I tried."

Nona looked between Will and the lapping water. Its surface was speckled with rain, but the reflection was still there, swirling and rolling, before solidifying once more. How could she help him? She couldn't just leave him here.

"If we could just hear what they were saying..." she said to herself in frustration. She squinted over the edge, trying to get a closer look.

"Nona, don't," said Castor, placing his hand on her shoulder. "It's the lake. Don't let it draw you in too."

Castor was right. His words and touch acted like a spell and Nona stepped away from the water immediately. But she still had to do something... Could the glass help her? Give her a vision or some sort of a clue? She was willing to try anything. She pulled it from her pocket, unwrapped it and looked through it at the man in front of her.

Many images at once flashed across its surface. Nona could hardly fathom it all. A baby. A boy in shorts and covered in dirt, making mud pies. A boy picking bluebells for his mum. A man working in an office. Laughing with friends. Dancing with his sweetheart.

All were Will. Of his life before the war. He was a person like any other – with his own mind and hopes, his own life – before the war came along. Did he need reminding?

Nona put the glass away and gasped. Will was deteriorating fast. In moments he would become stone completely. As she watched, the sparkle of quartz climbed up his chin, his cheeks, touched his lips…

"Stop," said Nona. She leaped forwards and grabbed his shoulder. All that could move of him now were his eyes, and their attention flickered for the first time, ever so slightly, towards Nona.

At that moment Nona felt something surge through her – and jump into Will. It was an unfamiliar feeling, like flexing a muscle she didn't know she had. It felt natural.

The stone had stopped spreading – for now. But how to reverse its effects? She felt it had to rest on convincing Will… His mind had trapped him here. Perhaps it could also set him free. "I think I understand," she told him. "You're trying to find out your fate from the lake. But the more you sit here, the more this *becomes* your fate."

Will's head began to turn, very slightly, towards Nona. She went on.

"You think your friends want you to join them, or that you should have died with them or something – but they would have wanted you to live. I'm sure of it! None of this is about who deserved it and who didn't. No one deserved it." There was a resonance to her voice that hadn't been there before. It seemed to echo through her body like a hum, travel along her arm and deep into Will. "Remember them," said Nona. "But move on. Try to remember who you are."

Tears that she couldn't explain rolled down Nona's cheeks. And her heart ached. For Will, yes. But also for her own mother and brother. For all the time she'd spent feeling the same way as Will.

All of Will's rock-like qualities had gone now. And a change came over his face as he gazed up at her. A light shone in his eyes – through his skin. Nona realized he was looking younger by the second. Almost as youthful as his reflection in the lake.

Was this spirit magic? How was it possible that Nona had performed such a thing?

Slowly, Will stood. His reflection in the water retreated. The faces of his friends rippled, swirled, and were gone. He wobbled on his feet unsteadily and had to use his arms for balance. Then he seemed to get the hang of it.

"I haven't been on my feet in an age," he said, staring at his boots and smiling. He clasped Nona's arms and beamed. "All this time, the past has been killing me," he said. His voice was hoarse, and his eyes sparkled with tears. "You've set me free. I don't know how. But you did."

Nona couldn't help feeling proud. But mostly she felt relieved. That she'd done something. That, after all this time, Will had broken free from the lake's bewitchment.

"It's all well and good to chat, but it's getting even darker now, Nona," said Castor. "We should get back. Quickly." Nona nodded and turned to Will.

"I must hurry back to my family too," said Will. "I'd all but forgotten them. When you stare into that water everything else is lost to mist."

Will took off the knapsack that had been slung over his shoulder, rummaged around inside and pulled out a tobacco tin. It opened with a popping sound and a warm, leathery smell flooded out. Inside was loose tobacco and a small pack of matches. Will handed the matches to Nona. "Take these," he said. "If you ever need me, just light a candle."

"Thank you." Nona wasn't sure how doing that could possibly help her, or in what situation she might need him, but she appreciated the kindness.

Will gave Nona a warm kiss on the forehead. She blushed and turned quickly so that Will wouldn't see, then she and Castor set off back the way they'd come. It was only when they reached the edge of the clearing that Nona realized she hadn't collected the one thing she'd come for: the lake water. What a scatterbrain.

How could she forget? She tutted at herself.

"Wait, Castor." She caught him by the arm and turned back towards the lake, towards Will…

Just in time to see Will turn translucent and fade into thin air. The waters of the lake were perfectly still. There was no sign that anyone had been there with them at all.

24

Nona staggered in disbelief. She'd spoken to Will. Felt his touch. Surely he'd been real. Surely he couldn't have been a phantom all along. A mere echo of the past...

Castor squeezed Nona's shoulder. "That's not normal. Let's get out of here," he said. The tremble in his voice told her that she wasn't the only one who'd been caught off-guard. Though she couldn't yet find the words to speak, she reached up to place her hand on his, and gripped it hard. Her mind whorled. She scanned the whole clearing for another glimpse of Will, but he just wasn't there.

She had proof he'd been real, though, didn't she? His pack of matches. Nona took her hand away from Castor's and pulled the matches out of her pocket. They were an older brand, the box battered and tatty and flecked with dirt. She was sure the pack had been new when he'd given it to her a moment ago.

"What in the *worlds* are you doing here?"

Nona spun round to face the person who'd spoken. The last of the daylight gleamed off Serafin's golden shawl and the strands of silver in her black hair. It hurt Nona's eyes. Hovering just a step behind Serafin like a shadow was Alesea.

"Well?" asked Serafin. Her eyes blazed, though her voice was steady. "Why have you come here even after I impressed upon you how dangerous this place is?"

"Castor, you were supposed to be keeping an eye on her, to make sure she stayed at the mill house," said Alesea from behind Serafin, her eyes narrow.

"I did keep an eye on her," Castor muttered. "Just not in the right place."

"Serafin, I—" began Nona. But she couldn't get her words out. What had happened with Will just now had been too overwhelming. Instead she ran and buried her face against the spirit's stomach.

Serafin froze, and Nona could sense her taking in the situation: Nona and Castor, here at the lake; the water flask in Nona's hand, still empty.

Serafin took the flask from Nona, as if relieving her of a burden, and she felt Serafin's arms slowly encircle her. "We saw someone just now," Nona blubbed. "We spoke to him just over there. But he disappeared."

Serafin sighed deeply. It sounded like a soothing gust of wind through the trees. When she pushed Nona away by the shoulders, gently but firmly, she crouched level with her. "This is no place for you. Either of you." She shot Castor a look and carried on. "Lost ghosts gather here. Ones who haven't yet found their way to the spirit paths that lead to the otherworld. They can become trapped, and change. I wouldn't be surprised if that's what you saw."

Is that what Will had been? A lost ghost? Now she thought of it, his uniform had been pristine – as though he'd put it on fresh yesterday. She'd just accepted it, what with everything else going on. The magic. The turning to stone and all. But the war had been over for years and he'd looked as though he'd stepped right out of it. She'd been years too late to be of any real help to Will.

"I thought I could rescue him. But he was already gone," said Nona. Her face felt sticky and hot, and embarrassment mixed with all the other feelings as she tried to hide her face behind her hair. But she could feel Castor standing close by, and that gave her strength. "He said he was going back to his family, but ... that wasn't true, was it?"

Serafin looked over her shoulder to Alesea and shrugged. "This is your realm, Alesea," she said. "You talk to her."

Alesea hesitated. "You did help him, Nona," she said at last. She still wore her hood pulled up around her face, and the plucked flowers that adorned her hair had started to wilt, Nona noticed. The petals looked papery and translucent.

Alesea's grey-green eyes fixed on Nona's. "You showed him the way," Alesea said. "No doubt you calmed him too." Her voice was soothing, although her eyes remained cold, as if still weighing Nona up. "It's something I used to take pride in doing before *his* power strengthened and I was forced to hide."

"It doesn't make sense. Why do *I* have that power, if I'm a human?" asked Nona.

Alesea and Serafin shared a glance, but neither of them spoke. Nona's stomach turned. There was something they weren't telling her – something important. She stepped back from both of them and stopped when her shoulder brushed Castor's. Her body felt heavy with grief now – not just for Will, but for her own lost family. All she wanted to do was curl up on her mother's lap, surrounded by her familiar scent, and sleep. Why was she – a human – able to do *their* magic? Why was it her – Nona – who had to face the Soldier?

It struck her that she was standing on the bank of a lake that showed the onlooker prophecies. What had Serafin called them? *Terrible truths*. About the future or the past. Suddenly Nona felt she couldn't go on any longer without knowing.

She inched towards the lake. The expressions on Alesea and Serafin's faces changed. They had guessed what she was up to. Serafin surged forwards but Alesea held her back.

"Stop, darling Nona. Please," said Alesea in her soft, lulling voice. Even so, urgency pierced through the false sugary-sweetness.

"Don't look into the water, Nona," warned Serafin. "We don't know what it could do to you." She reached out a hand towards Nona – an offering for her to take.

"You're trying to keep the truth from me," said Nona, looking from one to the other. "You have been for a long time. But if you won't tell me why I can do spirit magic, or why I've got to face the Soldier, then I'll have to find out for myself, won't I?"

"Do not do it," said Serafin. "Nona, it could kill you, as it does the rattlesticks. I'm telling you the truth." The spirits edged towards her, as if approaching an animal that might startle.

"Why?" demanded Nona. "*Why* could it kill

me? What do *I* have in common with rattlesticks? Tell me!"

"Nona, I don't know if this is a good idea," said Castor. He looked anxious, caught in the growing space between Nona and the two spirits. "I don't know what the water'll do. I'm as in the dark as you about all this. But is it worth the risk? We saw what it did to Will with our own eyes…"

Nona stepped closer to the water lapping at the black bank.

"All right," cried Alesea, reaching out a pale hand, "Please, stop. I'll tell you what I can. You defied *death*, Nona. On the night your family were killed, you were supposed to be taken too. I had come to show you the way." The smile Alesea usually wore had vanished, replaced by an anguished knitted brow. "Serafin was with me to tend any wounded. But you chose your own path. Only one other has done such a thing."

"If you look into the water," warned Serafin, "it could restore you to the destiny you escaped that night. Just as it shows the rattlesticks what they truly are. You defied death, child. We don't know how the water will affect you. The Soldier survived it, but he has infinitely more power than you to protect him."

Nona's mind raced. The Soldier had been here too? Is this where he'd seen the prophecy about her?

And she had been supposed to die with the rest of her family. She'd spent years feeling guilty for surviving when they didn't. What did this make her? Something unnatural? A monster, like the Soldier?

No. She was alive. That meant she wasn't like the rattlesticks – or the Soldier. Her body was flesh and bone. Her heart beat. More than ever she had to know what happened on the night her mother and brother were killed.

The spirits came towards her both at once, their arms outstretched. But Nona was at the lake's edge already.

She spun around and fixed her gaze on her reflection in the still, deep waters.

25

An icy shock of cold pierced through Nona, as if she'd plunged head first into the water – but she hadn't. Had she? Everything was muddled in her head. Her body felt frozen with cold and when she tried to move, her limbs resisted as if she were underwater. Her skull ached like it would split from the pain. She struggled to heave breath into her lungs. How could she be drowning when she sat on solid ground?

Everything around her had faded to grey. It was just her – and the reflection in the lake. But it wasn't only a reflection. It felt as though she was *inside* it, as well as looking down at it.

Her old living room swam into shape around her. Everything from the pale yellow flowers of the wallpaper to the net curtains hanging in the dark windows was the same. The tasselled lampshade by the threadbare armchair and the small square dining table at the centre of the room. Even the faint smell of roast potatoes, and her mother's dried lavender and rose petal scent pots. She could see the half-heart glass, leaded in and whole, glinting pink in the window.

It was night, and a seven-year-old version of herself slumbered with her mother on the sofa under a woollen blanket. Nona could see the shapes of their bodies – hers and her mother's – huddled together, their breath rising and falling. They'd taken to sleeping there, she remembered, because they thought it was safer than the bedroom, and they would be quicker getting to the building's cellar. Her brother slept behind the bureau.

Nona breathed in the smell of the place – immersed herself in it. Now that she was here, perhaps she could stay for ever...

Suddenly from all around came the sound of the air-raid siren. The noise of it turned Nona's stomach to lead. A deafening bang and rumble made the ceiling and the floor shudder. The tremors ran up her legs. Ripples ran out around her, and in an instant Nona remembered that this was nothing but a vision of what had once been. A cry lodged inside her throat. She didn't want to see it, and yet she felt compelled to.

In the scene around her, Nona's younger self

woke. Before her mother could stop her she'd crossed to the centre of the room. Every part of it was familiar. Before now she'd only remembered the briefest flashes; the scent of burning; flying shards of glass. And yet just watching it play out awakened her memory. Had the lake's magic dredged these images from her own mind? It must have done.

And she dreaded what would come next.

Another violent explosion shook the room. "Mum?" That was her brother's voice from behind the bookcase.

"It's all right, Amos," said Nona's mother. "We've not been hit yet, but let's get downstairs as quickly as we can. Nona, come back where I can keep an eye on you." Her mother sounded calm and defiant. But the bombing had always made Nona want to run. She remembered that now.

Nona thought she might be sick. All this felt like a forgotten film, playing back. Like watching a disaster unfold in the same way, for the hundredth time, and yet still not being able to anticipate what comes next.

Perhaps if she acted now – if she made a dash to the bureau and dragged Amos to safety – she could at least save her brother. But this was the past. How could she save him? Still, she cried out with all her might. Her voice blanched as if in a strong gale – or underwater. No one could hear her.

The biggest explosion yet rocked through the room. A terrible tearing, grating, crunching sound tore through Nona's senses. The whole back of the room collapsed. Chunks of plaster and dust flew everywhere.

Nona was about to cry out again. Nobody would have heard her through the sound of collapsing rubble – the shattering of the windows that shredded the curtains… But her younger self beat her to it. She was screaming something. What was it?

Just one word. "STOP!"

And then everything did. Everything stopped, at once. Glass and debris hung in the air. Some of it caught the light and sparkled like snow. The air felt full of tension, like electricity. The glass and rubble seemed to vibrate – as if trying to release itself from its frozen state. Nona gasped. She could see now what her younger self had. The thing that had made her cry out. Two watchful faces reflected in one of the shards of glass.

Alesea. Serafin.

And not just any glass, but *the* glass. Her half-heart.

A cool breeze ruffled Nona's hair. As if it had been pushed away by an invisible force, the glass shards made a bloom of empty space at the centre of the room. And there, silhouetted in front of seven-year-old Nona, rising from the shadows in the gap it left, stood the spirits.

It was Serafin who spoke first, to Alesea. "What has happened? How has the child done this?"

Alesea looked down at Nona, horrified. "She's seen us, sister. Without even knowing what she was doing she called on the spirit world for sanctuary. That's how." She stared around at the frozen room, stepping in close to Serafin's side. Nona's mind whirred. How could this be true? How could she have frozen time itself?

"This little one? Done all this?" said Serafin, who seemed confused and irritated all at once. She didn't wait for a response from Alesea. To Nona, she said. "Go with Alesea, child. There is no need to worry. She will take great care of you and see that you are guided to the otherworld. There will be many of you," she added quietly. "Sadly, it's not my magic that is required on this night."

"No," said the young Nona. She balled her fists and stood firm. "I won't!" She roared a child's fierce, wordless bellow of defiance.

The mighty Serafin took a small step back and glanced nervously at Alesea.

"We can't make her," murmured Alesea. She looked even paler than usual, and her face wore no smile. "If this girl demands our sanctuary we have no choice but to give it. She's already slipped one foot into our world, sister. It happened the moment she saw us in the glass," she said. Awe and fear seemed to mingle on her face. "I never thought this could happen again, in spite of what the prophecy told us. Or that it would be a small child! She can't be the one, can she? How could she hope to save us all from the Soldier? No, something must be wrong…"

"I know you're talking about me dying," said the young Nona. "I might be a kid, but I'm not daft. And I won't go with you, no matter what you say. Me and Mum and Amos are staying here where we belong!" She roared at them again to show she meant it – an outpouring of fear and resistance.

Serafin raised an eyebrow, but still didn't speak to Nona directly. "She is fierce," she said. "Perhaps she could be the one to end all this. Perhaps she is the one prophesied to defeat him. We will need to protect her until she's ready. Otherwise she will fail, as the prophecy tells."

"I just can't believe that this tiny little girl…"

"Alesea. Sister. She stands in front of us plain as day. We *must* believe it."

Alesea stepped towards Nona. The glass shards and rubble moved out of her way as she did, so they never once touched her. The young Nona stood rigid and breathing hard. Alesea's eyes were red-rimmed and watery, but in an instant she'd masked her fear and sadness with a smile. The young Nona bared her teeth.

"Don't worry, darling," said Alesea to Nona. "I can't force you to come with me now that you've seen us. Neither of us can. It seems you've outwitted your destiny to die this day. But don't be fooled." Alesea's smile fell as she moved closer and a tremble rose in her voice. "Your new destiny is more fearful than the last. Perhaps you will come to regret it. Be well," she said. "We'll meet again one day. Until then my little spell will make sure that no vision he has can reveal your face." In a single gliding move, Alesea touched Nona's cheek gently and whispered something.

Then the women were gone, taking Amos and her mother with them.

What followed was a chaos of noise, sound and movement. Crunching, crashing, darkness. Billowing dust that obscured Nona's vision.

The last thing Nona saw as everything imploded was the half-heart glass, with its fresh gleaming edge reflecting moonlight, flying across her young self's cheek and leaving a cut.

26

"NONA? NONA!" NONA COULD HEAR CASTOR calling her name and feel someone shaking her shoulders. Everything was dark. She flailed around, trying to find her bearings, but in her panic nothing made sense.

Then, all at once, the world came flooding back. Nona gulped down a deep breath. She flung out her arms to steady herself and found the grass beneath her, the sky above. She lay on the bank. Castor, Alesea and Serafin were gathered around, their anxious faces pressed close to hers. She let out her breath.

That last image stuck in her mind: the half-heart glass through which she'd first seen the spirits. The thing that had cut the younger Nona. *Her.* She touched her own face. Felt with trembling fingers the familiar ridge of the scar down her cheek. Remembered how she'd come round with the glass in her hand, and ever since then she'd seen glimpses of things that shouldn't be possible. She knew now that Alesea was responsible for her scar. Her spell had hidden Nona's identity from the Soldier all this time.

"Nona, you could have been killed," shouted Serafin. "What were you thinking?"

"You saw what happened. Didn't you?" said Alesea, studying Nona. "The Soldier pieced together every memory I'd hidden from him too, in his visions. And when he was drawn to this lake ten days ago, he saw the prophecy about you. Although your face was clouded by my spell." It was hard to read Alesea's expression: she looked fearful and excited, all at once. Maybe even a little ashamed.

Nona didn't respond to either of them. When she could finally find the energy to speak again it was to ask, "Why?"

After a silence it was Serafin who answered, in a much calmer tone this time. "When you glimpsed us and cried out, you invoked the sanctuary of the spirit world. It meant you would be safe. And," she went on, "it means you have a foot in both worlds now. That is why you have some magic. Why you can see us. Your half-heart became enchanted, since that is how you first saw us. It connected you to our world. As the Soldier's glass heart did for him."

"That's not what I meant," said Nona, struggling to her feet and backing away. "Why did you let Mum and Amos die?" She could feel the anger building inside, making her voice quiver.

Serafin and Alesea glanced at each other.

"It was too late for them, Nona," said Alesea finally. "We don't have that power."

"You *knew* I meant for us *all* to be safe. You didn't tell me they would die anyway." Her chest felt tight. With grief. With rage.

"It was only you who saw us, darling," said Alesea. "Only you who stood between the worlds in that precious moment. I guide the dead, comfort them. Serafin gives the wounded a fighting chance with her powers. Neither of us can control human destiny. Please, listen."

"This is exactly why we kept it from you," said Serafin, folding her arms and casting her gaze to the sky. "We knew it would be too hard for you to understand." Her tone was angry, but Nona could tell she used it to mask her worry.

"It's happening like it did before," whispered Alesea, grabbing Serafin's arm. "She's turning against us like he did. What if she's not the one, sister? We knew there would be another like the Soldier who could defeat him – but we never learned *who*. What if we've made a terrible mistake?"

Nona glared at them in disgust. Was that what they thought of her? That she couldn't deal with the truth? That she would become like *the Soldier* now she knew what really happened, and try to steal back the lives of her mother and brother? Join forces with him, even?

And yet… She and the Soldier did seem bound together in ways not even Serafin and Alesea understood. Thoughts flitted through Nona's mind before she could seize any to study more closely. The only constant was her anger. It raged through her body like a whirlwind, disordering everything it touched.

Alesea and Serafin could not be trusted. They were spirits – they must have been able to do *something* for her family. There must have been some way to save them – if only she'd known what it was.

Perhaps the only way for Nona to find the truth of anything was to look for it herself. But she needed to get away from them first, so she could slow down her thoughts.

Nona glared at the spirits again, then finally held Castor's worried gaze. "I'm sorry," she said to him, before she turned and fled into the trees.

She dodged round twisted branches and ran over uneven ground. She hoped she wouldn't fall on a rock or twisted root and break a bone in the dusk. She'd transform into her second skin – become a wren – if only she could focus through her all-consuming anger. She'd had enough of all their lies and half-truths. Who were they really protecting her from? The Soldier, or themselves? They weren't blameless. They'd taken her mother and brother. Perhaps the Soldier was the only one who could understand. Perhaps he would understand her...

The spirits' calls quickly grew distant. Nona stopped, realizing she had no idea where she was going. She didn't hear the pounding of feet catching her up until they were right behind her.

A cold hand grabbed Nona's shoulder. The fingernails sank in. She screamed.

"It's OK. It's only me," came Castor's voice. Nona sank back on her heels as she turned to see his face, pressed close to hers. Her lungs ached from her run. Castor recovered from his sprint quickest, stretched out his back and stood tall. "They'll be here any minute," he said. "If you want to dodge them, we could fly, or..."

They looked around at the trees. What was it Alesea had told her? *Imagine yourself as part of it.*

Imagine yourself into it. Say these words: Let me through to the hidden path.

The shock of Castor's arrival seemed to have interrupted the turmoil inside Nona's mind. Perhaps she could calm herself enough to travel in the way Alesea did. It was worth a try. She placed her palm against the nearest tree and held her other hand out for Castor. He took it. Nona grinned and squeezed it tight, closed her eyes and felt the bark against her fingers. In spite of the cold all around, a warmth came from inside it, like a fire burning in the hearth behind a closed door.

"Let me through to the hidden path," Nona whispered. "Let me through..."

A rushing sound of wind filled her ears. Nona's vision misted green and grey. She reached out to steady herself, but found nothing to grab, and nothing beneath her feet.

All she had to keep her bearings was Castor's hand in hers. It felt as though she was falling through the sky to earth, from a great height. The rushing sound grew louder. She couldn't tell which way to go. She'd brought them here. How would she get them out?

"This way," said Castor, tugging her hand.

Squinting in the direction he pulled her, she thought she could see the outline of the umbrafell.

Uncle. She longed to see him again. Perhaps she should just go back to the church, find a way to get them both out of there and run from all this? But another thought swept her up and wouldn't let her follow. What if she faced the Soldier now and put an end to all this? What if she could reason with him, face to face? She knew what it was to lose the people you loved. Maybe he would see that. Nona felt the wind shift around her, and a new way opened: a path, as if of stone.

"Come on," insisted Castor and pulled at her hand again.

"No," Nona said. "This way." With effort, she turned in the direction of the new path.

Something shifted, as though she'd stepped out from the shade. The rushing of air all around them stopped. In its absence she toppled onto her knees.

Nona kneeled on damp grass. They were under a muddy, dusk sky, amid a cluster of spirit lights, and sleet had started to fall. It looked like ash raining down on them from a great bonfire. A darkling beetle wandered across the back of her hand as she caught her breath. She watched it make its slow path across her to find the other side.

"Still not sure I like that," said Nona, once she could speak again. "Does travelling that way get any easier?" Pressure and a loud rumbling in her ears lingered even now, as if she had water trapped in them. They were in a small crater of sunken earth surrounding an old standing stone – the one which they had undoubtedly travelled through.

Castor ignored her question, grabbed her face with his cold fingers so that she looked into his. Nona still hadn't got used to seeing him as a human boy.

"I didn't know anything about what happened to you, I swear," he said. "Alesea told me to keep an eye on you, but that's not why I stuck around. I did that because…" He glanced away. "I did it because you're my friend." Nona smiled. She wondered what colour he would have changed into that moment as an imp. Castor went on. "You believe me, don't you?' he said. "That I didn't know…"

"Yes, Castor. I do. Now let go. You're squeezing my head."

"Oh! Sorry." Castor whipped his hands behind his back.

Nona took a breath. "I've been thinking," she said.

"Oh no."

She half-scowled, half-smiled at his quip, before turning deadly serious again. What she had to say was difficult. And frightening. Every time she thought about it, her stomach turned as if she were at sea in a storm. But in spite of her terror, there was a calm, inner voice that said, *I'm so tired of running.* She swallowed hard.

"What if we summon the Soldier," she said.

Castor's face creased with disbelief. For a moment Nona thought he was going to turn into a crow and fly straight off. But instead he said, "Summon the Soldier? Are you joking?"

Nona sighed sharply. "All this running and hiding. It's not working, is it? And fighting the rattlesticks – all it does is wear everyone down. You've seen Serafin – she's strong, but even *she* is tired of all this. The rattlesticks just keep coming. Castor." She bent towards him, her voice lowered. "What if we bring the Soldier to us?"

"To kill him?"

"To speak with him."

"*Speak* with him?" Castor yelled. "Now I know you're joking."

"I have to understand my part in all this. There's no way I can fight someone that powerful. You know it and I know it. But what if I can talk him down? You saw what happened with Will. I've lost my family too, just like he has," she went on. "Perhaps he'll listen to reason."

"Reason?"

Nona stopped herself from calling Castor a parrot and instead fished around in her pocket for the glass fragment – her half-heart. She pulled off the collection of hankies and held it up between them. "I think I can do it with this," she said. "If what I saw in the lake is right, then glass doesn't just separate the worlds, it can connect them too. That's how I saw Serafin and Alesea. And it was through glass that the Soldier first saw the spirit world too." She remembered her vision the night she'd spent at Serafin's house. How the young officer – who she now knew was the Soldier – had lifted the drinking glass to his lips and glimpsed Alesea. That would have been the moment of his death, had he not seen her. And yet he'd defied his destiny – just like Nona.

"It would explain all my dreams when I'm near the glass," she added. "Castor. I'm going to try."

Nona stopped and stared. Through the slightly warped, rose-coloured glass, Castor looked perfect in every way. Not chisel-jawed, know-it-all and virtuous perfect. But just exactly what he was. Messy, confused, certain, arrogant and brave, scared and loving, ever-changing and ever the same. Perfectly himself. Human. In that moment she wished more than anything that he could look through the glass and see himself the way she could.

A smile crept over Nona's face – one that she realized she had seen Uncle Antoni wear many a time when he was looking at her. At the time she'd wondered what it meant.

Castor frowned and shifted. "What is it?"

"Nothing." Nona re-angled the glass.

Castor moved closer and placed his hand on her shoulder.

"Do you know what you're doing?" he asked. "I mean, I can call up a few rocks when I need something to throw and find my way through the stones, but that's about the sum of *my* magic."

"No," said Nona. "I haven't got a clue."

"Great," he said. "Neither have I. Let's do it."

They caught one another's eye and grinned anxiously. Nona's heart thumped loudly in her chest. She brought the glass closer to her face and gazed into it. *Soldier*, she said in her mind. *I know you can hear me. And I know you can sense me, because I can sense you. I'm here waiting. Come and find me.* She let the words fill her up, travel through every part of her. The glass began to cloud. To darken.

In response, Nona heard the unmistakable voice in her mind. *I can hear you, little mouse.*

Castor groaned with dread and stuffed his hand into Nona's pocket that held the stone.

Nona put down the glass and looked.

Beyond the dip where she and Castor stood, the ground levelled out into a wide, open plain. Only now they were beneath blue-black clouds that tapered down to earth in a funnel shape.

And directly under that stood the Soldier.

27

THE SOLDIER LOOKED LIKE A GIANT. HE HAD TO BE eight feet tall, at least. And the huge cape of black fur draped around his shoulders made him look even bigger. Like an oversized bear. Tattered black rags whipped around his ankles – the remnants of a second, former cape, perhaps. From his chest emanated the red glow Nona had glimpsed in her dreams: the glass heart.

He was far from the nervous young officer she'd seen in the glass, celebrating the liberation of a French town with his peers.

The Soldier's face was also covered – by a stag's skull. Part of his neck was visible, paler than the skull. The cavernous eyeholes looked right through Nona. It made her feel tiny.

And yet he didn't acknowledge Nona or Castor...

Of course, she realized. The pocketstone. He couldn't see her – or Castor while he touched it.

As if in response, the Soldier's voice came to her again, deep, resonant and foreboding. "I know you're here, little mouse," it said. "Show yourself. I know you're the one I'm looking for. I can sense your enchanted glass is with you." His voice had turned smug. "Now just let me see your face."

Nona checked around. The funnel-shaped winds surrounded the Soldier – standing between him and them. It looked violent enough to strip the flesh off their bones. But the standing stone was still within reach. If they needed to, they could use it to escape...

"There's a weather spell to help us get through the cyclone," whispered Castor. The freckles on his nose looked darker against his paling skin. "If I remember it right. You just raise your hands over your head, like this –" Castor created half a mini archway with one arm, as he was still holding onto Nona with the other – "and you say, *A pause, please, Mother Sky*. Have you got that?"

Nona grimaced. "I think so."

"Good. It'll get us through the cyclone to him. And back again." Castor bent and touched the earth with his free hand while keeping his other in Nona's pocket, and when he took it away from the ground a small pile of stones had gathered. Weapons. With his eyebrow raised, Castor stuffed the stones into his woollen jacket.

Although she hoped to reason with the Soldier, Nona was glad she still had the pointed branch she'd used to fend off rattlesticks in Serafin's woods, stuck through the straps of her rucksack.

"Little mouse," came the Soldier's voice. "You surely didn't call on me only to hide. Come closer."

The cyclone slowed, twisted and uncoiled. With a hiss, it faded into air. Clearing their path towards him.

"Wasn't expecting that," muttered Castor. "Don't like it." He gripped Nona's hand tighter.

Nona gulped, though her mouth and throat were dry. With a glance at Castor, she spoke. "You're right," she croaked. "I didn't call on you just to hide."

Nona's insides churned so much she thought she might vomit. Slowly, as if trying to creep up on a snake, Nona took a step towards the Soldier. Then another. And another. She had to drag her stiff legs to make them move. Castor, still with his hand in Nona's pocket, shuffled alongside her. It was so the stone would protect him too, but Nona knew he also kept close through fear, because she felt it too.

"Nona, think about this," Castor hissed, eyeing the standing stone behind them. "We could still escape." But Nona kept moving forwards. She'd come too far to back out now.

They were close enough to hear the Soldier's crackly breath and see the pale skin between the cape and the skull mask more clearly. Still Nona didn't reach for the pocketstone. Not yet.

"I've come to tell you that I don't mean you any harm," she said, one word bumping into the next in her hurry to get them out. As she spoke, she reached for her branch and began to draw it out. Just in case. "I don't want any more fighting. I'm sick to death of it. I think everyone is – the spirits too, by the sound of it. Do you remember what being human is like?" Nona finished drawing out the branch and brought it to her side. "If so, please will you listen to what I have to say?"

The Soldier was silent for a moment. Then he said, "I will listen, little mouse. Come here and show yourself."

All the while they were talking, Nona was reaching out slowly with the branch, towards the Soldier's chest. Her arms shook and her teeth chattered, but she couldn't help herself: she wanted so desperately to see the heart. It was the key to all his power. Might it also be the key to freeing him from his turmoil? He'd lost a child, just as she'd lost her family. If she freed him from his pain, he might see that stealing power from the spirits – and especially sacrificing Nona's life – was wrong.

If she could just touch the heart, as she'd touched Will's shoulder…

The stick was hard to wield with a trembling hand, so Castor grabbed hold of it too. Together they guided the end of it to the right place.

"I know you want to sacrifice me to bring your son back," Nona said. It was hard to speak through chattering teeth. "I've lost people too, so I know what it feels like. But the truth is they're gone." She couldn't help choking on the words. "Maybe there's some other way for me to help you," she added quickly, "where nobody else has to die. I've learned that I can heal…"

With the end of her branch, Nona and Castor drew aside the material covering the Soldier's chest – and they gasped as one.

The glass heart hung there, suspended in empty, inky blackness. It was … beautiful. It didn't move or function like an ordinary heart. It stayed perfectly still, glowing a deep, brilliant red. Inside it, something smouldered like a fire, pulsing slightly, and black smoke seemed to billow around, pressing against the glass sides and then retreating just as quickly.

That must be all of the Soldier's stolen power. The

heart both stored it and absorbed more from the world. There was just one piece missing – a gap on the left side. Through it, a steady stream of the smoke escaped.

That was why he needed her half-heart. Her enchanted glass – the only other like his. To complete his own.

None of that was what really shocked Nona, though. The heart itself was covered in beautiful patterns – fleur-de-lis and other elaborate designs. Like the pressed glass cup she'd seen the young officer drink from in her vision. The one through which he'd glimpsed Alesea – just as Nona had, through the half-heart. That's what he must have crafted it from.

"The missing piece is where the sniper's bullet struck first," the Soldier said. "When it missed." Nona held her breath, her stick still holding the Soldier's garments aside. "We thought we'd driven the enemy out, but one was waiting for us to let our guard down. The others were killed but I survived, because that's what I am. A survivor. I know you've seen what happened in your own morsel of magic." His eyes narrowed, though Nona knew he still couldn't see them because of the pocketstone.

"The spirits stole my memories, but a man of my intelligence can't be kept in the dark for long," he went on. "I worked it out. Just as I learned how to grow my power. Look closer, if you like. See exactly what you're up against."

As Nona stared into the heart, an image played across its surface. The Soldier, kneeling at a gravestone that must be his son's. Then it changed to him kneeling at the forbidden lake. Looking into the water. The prophecy he'd seen flashed in front of her – a torrent of images at once. She saw her half-heart in pieces, becoming forged with his – completing it. The rattlesticks rampaging through Serafin's home, stealing her magic. The sky in fast-forward; the first dawn of a waning moon. The Soldier and a girl inside the church together, beside the tree. Nona knew the girl was her, because she had on the same clothes – but where her face should be was just a blur. She saw herself, defenceless on the ground; he with his hands raised, drawing out her life...

Nona squeezed her eyes shut. She couldn't look any more. The Soldier had seen the time and the place of his victory. How could Nona hope to stop any of it?

"You see?" he said. "It is written. Everything will happen as it should."

Nona and Castor glanced at each other, and began to withdraw the stick.

Everything about the Soldier's demeanour changed. He grabbed Nona's branch and wrenched it from their hands. The fur of his cape fell across his heart again. With a roar the cyclone whipped once more, except this time Nona and Castor were inside it too. The Soldier turned towards them and looked down.

"Silly little mouse," he hissed. "Your spell must have worn off before you even called me here."

Nona dug her hand into her pocket and grabbed the pocketstone, but it cracked in her hand and crumbled to chalky dust.

The Soldier sneered. "Now I can see you with my own eyes and give your borrowed time to someone worthy of it. My son." He reached for them, his fingers rigid. Two rattlesticks began to rise beside him.

Nona clutched Castor and backed away but the wall of wind had closed in around them even tighter. The standing stone was a good sprint away on the other side...

With a yell that was as much fear as it was battle cry, Castor hurled the first of his stones at the Soldier – followed by another, and another. One whizzed past his shoulder. A second got lost in the fur of his cape. A third hit the Soldier's skull mask and left a tiny crack.

His stones used up, Castor transformed into a crow and dived at the Soldier's face, claws first.

"Castor, stop!" Nona yelled, but it was too

late. The Soldier knocked Castor down effortlessly. "Castor!" Nona cried again.

He fell at her feet with a sickly thud. One wing folded awkwardly against his body, the other open and ungainly. He lay stunned. Motionless. Nona hoped that was all it was. She quickly scooped him up.

The Soldier's rattlesticks moved towards them. With the wind wall closing in, there was so little space for Nona now. Small cries of panic escaped from her mouth as she whorled round, wondering what to do. Tightness gripped her lungs so she could hardly breathe. She knew only one thing: that she had to get both of them out.

She leaped to her feet and spun round to face the wind wall. "A pause, please, Mother Sky!" she shouted.

The archway she made with her arms was awkward and lopsided, because of the way she clutched Castor. Calm air opened up ahead of her just as he'd promised, but it was a mere sliver. Nona jumped into it, but not before the Soldier's fingers had closed around some of her hair. She yelped in pain and wrenched away from him, swallowing her cry as the wind closed behind her with a clatter.

It must have just clipped her ankle, because it sent her flying. The rattlesticks were obliterated in the wind. The ground came towards Nona abruptly. Just before she hit it, she twisted so that she didn't land on Castor and landed on her side instead. Something from her pocket crunched and its contents spilled onto the ground in pink fragments. *No.* Not her half-heart glass!

Behind her, the Soldier laughed. "It's happening just as I've seen," he said. "Now I have your power too, little mouse." The pieces lifted from the ground and levitated towards him. She just had time to grab one daggerlike shard before he took that too.

But there was no time to think about that now. All around her were more rattlesticks. If not in the process of rising, then fully formed and staggering towards her. She had to get on her feet – no matter how much it hurt. She couldn't fight this many rattlesticks herself, and if she didn't act now they'd have her trapped.

The quickest way to escape – the only way – was through the standing stone. She could make it in a few seconds – if she could find the strength to run. Castor squirmed and made a low, croaking sound. He was coming round, thank goodness – but he'd still be no help with the standing stone, and Nona needed to make an exit. Fast.

Nona scrambled to her feet. She ducked under the grasping arms of one of the rattlesticks, and narrowly missed another, which clacked its stone teeth right next to her ear.

With a burst of adrenalin, Nona sprinted away, out of the rattlesticks' reach. As she skidded into the dip of land surrounding the stone, she slapped her free hand against it. "Let me through to the hidden path," she said through gasps for breath. Nothing happened. She had to focus her mind.

The rattlesticks were getting closer. Behind them, the Soldier, at the centre of his cyclone of wind that stretched up into a thunderous black sky, held out a crooked hand towards her. She read such coldness in those hollow eye holes.

Nona pressed the side of her face against the rock. *Focus*, she thought.

"Let me through to the hidden path. Let me through to the hidden path. Let me through. Please," she begged. "Let me in." Her words resonated inside her. With her ear pressed against the cold stone, it seemed that she could hear her incantation echoing through it too.

She squeezed her eyes shut as three rattlesticks staggered into the ditch, their arms reaching for her. Nona hugged Castor tight to her chest.

A sudden heat travelled through her. As if the stone were a bath of warm water, and she was falling into it. When she opened her eyes, everything had turned grey. The rattlesticks were gone – and so was the Soldier. The familiar rushing in her ears drowned out every other sound.

But the Soldier's words lingered. *You can run, but you can't hide, little mouse. I've seen your face twice now. And I know where to find you again.*

28

NONA STUMBLED INTO GREY, BEWILDERING nothingness. There was only one thing on her mind: getting back to the church. To Uncle Antoni. To safety. An image sprang into her head of the umbrafell and she held onto it with all her might.

Pinpricks of light emerged from the grey now: paths leading in different directions. Everything else flickered, like the stilted, blinking images of the newsreels she'd seen during the war. Nona gasped. Down the path right in front of her, in the furthest distance, she could see the church emerging. All around the wind roared. Nona tried to walk towards the church, but clouds rolled in around it like moor mist, and moving became like trying to drag her legs through thick silt.

The feeling changed. The silt-like resistance

around Nona's legs shifted. Now it was a powerful undertow, dragging her away from her path and in an entirely different direction. She slipped and fell, still clinging to Castor. He stirred in her arms but fell silent again. What was happening? Would she be lost in this greyness for ever? All she knew was the tug of the undertow, dragging her towards a pinprick of light that grew larger, brighter, closer. And then flooded her vision from all sides.

Fresh, cold air filled her lungs. Nona gasped. She was on a hillside – she could tell by the coarse grass between her fingers, the tilt of the earth. The full moon hung bright and imposing in the night sky. Then she recoiled, her back pressing against cool stone – because a tall figure loomed over her. The Soldier?

As she blinked, her eyes grew more accustomed to the light. The towering silhouette became clearer.

Not the Soldier. Alesea. Her eyes flashing with anger.

"You've been consorting with our enemy, Nona," she said. "You'll pay for betraying our trust."

In seconds Nona felt too weak to stand. Alesea was draining her energy. And this time she was doing so on purpose.

"No," said Nona. "You don't understand."

An eagle owl swooped down from the sky and

landed behind Alesea. It carried something in its claws – what looked like a flask... *Nona's* flask. The owl seemed to unfurl in front of her eyes, growing ever bigger, until it became a crouching woman. Then the woman stood tall – her long black hair cascading over her feathered shawl. Serafin.

Alesea didn't even notice.

"You thought you could betray us," Alesea said, "after all we've done for you. You thought you'd join forces with him. We believed in you." Her lip quivered. Were there tears in her eyes? Nona feared what Alesea might do next. Dizziness made everything spin.

Serafin looked between them. Nona saw the realization of what was happening, the horror of it, dawn on her face in slow motion.

"Alesea!" she said, loud and firm. "Stop at once."

Alesea clenched her fist. Nona's lungs tightened.

"That's not it ... at all," Nona wheezed. "I wanted to make him listen, but ... he can't listen. I failed."

Serafin drew her staff to confront Alesea.

"Don't make me do this, sister." It was a warning – not a plea.

Nona let her shoulders sag in defeat. Her grip on Castor loosened and his wing flopped open. Alesea brought a hand to her mouth. The fury in her eyes turned to horror.

"Castor!" She fell to her knees and gathered Castor into her arms. All Nona's strength came rushing back, as though a heavy, crushing weight had been lifted.

A warm hand touched her face.

"Nona, are you all right?" asked Serafin, studying her closely.

"I—" Nona didn't know how to express all the things that were not all right. She'd put Castor in danger because she'd tried to reason with a monster. It was her fault he'd got hurt.

"He won't ever stop coming, will he?" Nona whispered. "The Soldier, I mean. Not until he gets what he wants. Or until he's stopped." She looked up into Serafin's eyes. Serafin gave a sombre nod.

"Come," she said, taking Nona's hand. "Castor needs help."

Castor was motionless in the cradle of Alesea's arms.

Serafin stepped forwards and in a gentle but commanding voice said, "Alesea. Allow me to see him." At first Alesea flinched from her, gathering Castor closer to her chest. Nona could see that her cheeks were tear-stained, her face contorted with grief. If ever Castor had doubted Alesea's love for him, Nona now knew the truth. It was obvious that she cared for him like a son.

Serafin held out her hand. "Alesea. It's me."

Still Alesea didn't speak, but she relaxed her grip on Castor.

Serafin crouched in front of her and laid her hands on him.

Nona approached Alesea and took Alesea's cold hand in hers. At first Alesea froze. Then she softened and gave Nona's hand the lightest squeeze. They stayed that way, in silence, for a long time.

Suddenly Castor moved his beak and squawked. With a rustle, he righted himself on Alesea's lap. Alesea wept and touched his face, but her smile was back. A true one.

"Castor," sighed Nona. "You're all right!"

He shook himself and studied her through one eye. By the way he kept his foot curled up under him, she could see it was badly hurt.

"Never better," he squawked, bobbing his neck and then throwing back his head in a crow laugh.

Nona smiled. Certainly as sarcastic as ever.

Alesea lowered her head. "I'm sorry, Nona," she said in a choked voice. "I thought..."

"No," said Nona. "I'm sorry. I should have listened to you both. I was angry."

Castor tested his wings. The powerful gust of wind they created blew back Nona's hair and made her eyes water. At least there was nothing wrong with those. Next, he shuffled on the spot, his one bad foot curled up under him, and began to contort himself into a ball. But he didn't become human again as Nona expected. He turned back into an imp. He patted himself down, confused.

"What's happening?" he asked. "Why am I like this when the full moon's still out?"

Alesea and Serafin glanced at each other, worried.

"It could be your injury," said Alesea. "Or something interfering with my magic…"

Nona looked down at the half-heart glass in her hand – or the thin sliver of what remained. She felt broken. The half-heart glass had been with her since the night her mother and brother died. It had felt like a part of her past. A part of *her*, full stop.

Now it was gone.

"It's him. The Soldier's the one interfering with your magic. He's got the half-heart," said Nona, the panic welling up inside her. "I couldn't stop him taking it – well, most of it – and now he's more powerful than ever. I saw the prophecy in his heart. Draining my life in the umbrafell on the dawn of a waning moon. That's tomorrow," she gasped, finally understanding. Then, remembering the other part of her vision, another thought struck her. "Serafin, you're here and it's night. What about your home? The rattlesticks will be—"

"Yes, they will be ransacking what power they can while I'm gone," she said quietly. "There's nothing that can be done about that now."

Nona's heart sank in despair. It was all happening – just as she'd seen. Just as the Soldier had promised. "It's all my fault, I—" But she couldn't go on.

An awful silence settled over them all.

Through tears, Nona studied the remaining piece of her half-heart. Its edges seemed to gleam golden when she angled it. At least she'd clung onto this one small piece. She wrapped it in the hankies with care, so that it wouldn't break through and cut her. What good could it do now that it was broken? Still, she couldn't stand to get rid of it.

"The main thing is we're back together," said Serafin, hands on her hips beneath her golden shawl and looking at each one of them in turn. "And together we can still fight – and win. Nothing is certain until it's done." She gave Nona a bright smile. For the first time Serafin's grit seemed to have been replaced with something lighter and more hopeful. Nona felt the spark of it leap into her, lift her own heart.

But the feeling didn't last. "I have to get back to the church," she said. "Right away. The Soldier said he knows where to find me. He's seen me twice now and the last time was at the church… If I'm right he'll be heading straight there."

"It's not finished," gasped Alesea. "The umbrafell won't be safe until we've sealed it with magic, and that can't happen until it's fully restored. You aren't ready for this. Don't go."

"I have to." Nona stepped back. The rain was hammering them now. She was drenched, and her old holey jumper, her brother's jumper, sodden with water, had stretched halfway down her thighs, pulling on her shoulders. "I can't leave Uncle Antoni."

Nona knew what she'd seen in the Soldier's glass heart. Him, winning. Stealing her life inside the very church that was supposed to protect her. But she couldn't not go back. She couldn't let Uncle Antoni get hurt.

Serafin straightened and drew in her breath. "Then we all go with you. Together we'll find a way." She strode towards Nona. Castor became a crow, squawked and flitted to her shoulder.

Only Alesea hung back. She stepped into shadow.

"Alesea?" said Serafin. They all turned to stare at her.

"I'm sorry," Alesea said. "I can't go with you."

29

Even through her own shock, Nona could tell that both Castor and Serafin were hurting more. Neither of them seemed able to move – or speak. "Alesea, please," said Serafin finally. "We – I – need your help."

Alesea shook her head and backed away further.

"Don't be frightened, Alesea," said Nona. Her voice sounded smaller and more childlike than ever, though she went on. "If we work together, like Serafin says, we might find a way..."

But Serafin spun round to face Nona and Castor. "It's fine," she said, although her face looked drawn, her eyes wide. She seemed smaller to Nona somehow. "You two go on ahead," she said. "I will talk to Alesea. If I can, I'll bring her with me." She gave them a weak smile. "Take this," she said, handing Nona her old water flask – the one she'd left with Serafin at the lake. It was heavy and made a sloshing sound when she took it. "It's lake water," said Serafin. "Perhaps it may be useful. Now go. Quickly. I'll be right behind you."

A stormy darkness that thickened the night had drawn in over the moors by the time Nona and Castor got close enough to see the church. The sky was laden with cloud that consumed the moon and continued to work its way down upon them. Was it the Soldier's doing? Nona felt sure he was using his newfound power to interfere with Alesea's moon magic.

They had flown to the nearest standing stone only to find it guarded by rattlesticks. No doubt there were more stalking around the most likely travelling trees and stones. The Soldier had seen Nona disappear into one of them, of course. This must have been his way of cornering her.

She remembered what Alesea had told her: that not even the Soldier could move through the stones and trees as they could. That was something, at least.

Instead, Nona and Castor flew side by side – he in his crow form and she as a wren. She could feel her tiny bird heart palpitating with the thrill of zipping and diving through the air. Nothing had ever felt so natural to her as flying over the rise and fall of the dark moors, lit only by shafts of golden storm light. Yet now wasn't the time to get carried away. She had to stay focused. Reach the umbrafell as fast as she could. Get to her uncle – before the Soldier got there first. Nona hoped against hope that he wasn't already waiting for her... But she'd seen it all play out at dawn. She knew that's when he'd attack.

Tiny as it was, she still had her sliver of the half-heart. So the Soldier's power wasn't yet absolute. She wondered if he'd foreseen that? If not, did it mean they still had a chance?

Nona scanned the horizon. Between the dark clouds of the sky, a thick white mist rolled in over the moors. It was creeping over the peaks of hills and flooding the valleys at a terrifying pace. It came from all around. Encircling them. Hiding everything from view.

Nona knew that, hidden in the mist, the Soldier was closing in. This had to be his tactic – to conceal his progress, his position, until the very last minute.

They saw the church from far off. The light spilling from inside gave it away. But as they came closer, it seemed that all was not well. The building no longer wore a cloak that made it look like an innocent wreck. And the smaller windows were all fitted along the side that Nona could see, but the large end window was still an empty space. The umbrafell was incomplete, as Alesea had said, its protective magic not yet built to its fullest. Without it, the spell that would stop the Soldier from entering, that would give safety to those inside – would be useless.

They drove on as fast as they could, until Nona's ribcage felt fit to burst.

Nona surged forwards, her wings a blur, while Castor seemed to glide effortlessly, his wings taut against the air currents that were buoying him, the long, elegant feathers upturned at the ends. They were directly over the church now.

Nona plunged towards the hatch and Castor followed. As they dived through it, they came face to face with a man – one of the tradespeople – who looked even more surprised than they were. The man noticed them at the last second. Nona caught sight of the fearful look in his eyes just before he swung his fists at them. But Nona was swift and dodged with ease, while Castor glided through out of range. Once inside, Nona transformed into her human self.

The man whisked round to stare at them. He held his fists in front of him. "Stay back," he shouted. Then, "What are you? How—"

So, Alesea had lifted the spell on them. But did it also mean that she had abandoned them all – and her hope along with them? Or, just as terrible, was this the Soldier's power, eclipsing hers? Nona exchanged a worried look with Castor. Could the Soldier ever be stopped, with or without the umbrafell?

"We're here to help. What do you remember?" said Nona. She held up her palm towards the frightened man to try to calm him. To show him she meant no harm.

The man lowered his fists a fraction. "All I know is I just … came round about half an hour ago, and here I was with all these other people."

"You've been under a spell," Nona said. "But something much worse is coming. The Soldier." She ignored the cold shiver that ran down her back as she spoke his name. "Our only chance now is to finish the last window – and to seal its magic. For us all."

Castor nodded. "Just let us go downstairs, all right?" he said. "We'll explain everything."

"Why should I let you?" the man stammered, directing his words at Nona. "How do I know you and that *thing* aren't dangerous?"

"My uncle will vouch for me," said Nona. "Uncle Antoni."

"Antoni?" The man straightened a little and the wild look in his eyes lessened. "Are you the one who wrote him that letter?" Nona nodded. He thought for a moment, and then jutted out his chin.

"Well? What are you waiting for? Get on with you." Nona didn't waste any time. She gave the workman a nod and streaked down the ladder to the upper floor, then the stone steps, with Castor clinging tight to her shoulder.

What faced her on the lower floor was pandemonium.

"Jenny Wren? Is that you?" Uncle Antoni, who stood at the centre of the throng, froze when he saw her. He was haggard and drawn, but alert.

"Uncle!" Nona ran down the final steps and across the room to him. She flung herself into his arms and squeezed. It really was her uncle. Safe and sound – and no longer bewitched.

"I got your note," he said into her shoulder. "I could hardly believe it. But what other explanation was there? I've felt like I've been trapped in a dream. Nona, you're frozen." He pulled away and looked her up and down. And it was as though the cold had finally caught up with Nona, because she couldn't stop shivering

"We've got worse problems," said Castor.

Uncle Antoni jumped back and stared at Castor, as if only just noticing him. "What—"

"That's Castor," said Nona through chattering teeth. "He's a friend." Nona smiled at Castor. Although he shifted uncomfortably under Uncle Antoni's gaze, he remained in his imp form. It must have taken a lot of courage to show himself like that.

For some moments, Uncle Antoni was silent. His face flushed, as if he was having trouble breathing, and Nona could see that he was grinding his jaw. This had to be hard on him. It wasn't every day you discovered you'd been under a spell, and got to meet an imp, Nona supposed. But then he straightened, and said in his calmest voice, "A pleasure to meet you, Castor." They shook hands.

Uncle Antoni continued, "But I have to ask. What do you mean, worse problems?" There was a pause before the pair of them burst into peals of laughter. Nona stared at them. All the fright and apprehension and disbelief flowed out of them in fits of giggles. She never could understand how Uncle made instant friends. "Finding out that I've been bewitched is plenty, thank you."

Now Nona turned her attention to all the people who had been released from Alesea's spell and were coming to terms with what had happened to them. They had no idea what they would be up against next. The Soldier. How would she break it to them?

A *thump* and a kerfuffle came from the floor above them. Uncle Antoni and Castor fell silent. Even over the uproar all around them they could hear the noise and chaos from above. There were raised voices – that of a man and a woman.

"It's Serafin," said Castor. "You mark my words. Bet she's run into our friend up there and given him another fright." He chuckled.

Nona held her breath and waited. Sure enough, it was Serafin who came running down the stairs. People covered their eyes against her dazzling light. From her gleaming golden wing shawl to her proud stature, anyone could tell there was something special about her.

She scanned the room and found Nona, who squinted at her hopefully as the ache in the back of her eyes subsided. But it was Castor who spoke.

"Alesea?" he asked.

Serafin shook her head.

Nona didn't have to look at Castor's changing colour to know he felt as disappointed as she did. Except for Castor it would have had an added hurt. She reached up and stroked his scaly back.

Uncle Antoni looked between them with a frown of concern. Though no one but Nona noticed, he couldn't keep the astonishment out of his eyes.

"There was no persuading her," Serafin said. "She's made her decision."

Nona surveyed the church. Serafin must have caught her looking, because she said, "You'd better explain to these people what's going on."

"She's right, Jenny Wren," said Uncle Antoni. He placed a warm hand on her shoulder. "You need to explain. If we're still in danger they all need to know."

30

NONA MADE HER WAY THROUGH THE JOSTLING bodies to the raised altar at the back of the church with Castor on her shoulder. From there she tried to get everyone's attention.

No one was listening.

Over in the corner, Uncle Antoni stood awkwardly next to Serafin, and watched.

Nona tried bellowing at the top of her voice again to call for hush. If anyone heard, they ignored her.

"That's it. I've had enough," grumbled Castor. "All these people in my house. And they can't even be bothered to listen..." Nona felt his transformation on her shoulder without having to look. In seconds his sharp crow talons were digging into her shoulder.

"Craaw!" Castor pushed off and sailed around the rafters, swooping low over people's heads and circling

again. He neared the side wall, then transformed mid-air into an imp and clung to the stonework, scampering. Then he leaped into the air and became a crow again.

That got people's attention. Someone cried out in fear. Everyone drew away from the windows and huddled together at the centre of the room.

Now that he'd made his presence known, Castor glided to where Nona stood and landed neatly on her shoulder once more. Serafin caught Nona's eye and smirked. People were certainly listening now.

"I know this won't be what you want to hear and that you probably all want to go home to bed," Nona shouted to the assembled crowd. "But something is about to attack. Something called the Soldier." She grimaced just at the thought of him. His giant stature. His skull mask. Would this all be over if she just gave herself up? Could she save the others, if she did? Perhaps the Soldier's vision of the prophecy had to come true, and then, for the rest of the world at least, everything would go back to normal…

Nona surveyed them all. She remembered what Serafin had told her at the mill house and what little she'd seen of the Soldier herself. She knew in an instant that he'd never stop coming. Given the chance, he'd turn every living thing into a rattlestick.

"It's me he wants," Nona said more quietly. "He's going to try to kill me, and I have to stop it. I'm the only one who can. *If* I can," she muttered. She looked around. "But I don't believe he cares who he hurts on the way."

"Then what do we do?" said one person.

"Get as far away from here as possible," said another.

"You could," said Nona. Her throat felt tight. Get as far away from *her* as possible, they may as well have said. "But the Soldier could be anywhere in that mist out there. I don't believe you'll be safe. I'm sorry you all got drawn into this, but our best bet is to stay together. I – *we* – need your help, to finish the last window." Most of the attention turned to the workbench where pieces of glass lay scattered and only the lower half had been fixed temporarily into lead with horseshoe nails. "Once this place is finished it'll make the magic inside it strong. Then we –" she looked towards Serafin – "can make a spell that'll stop the Soldier getting inside. And we'll be safe, until I work out a way to stop him for good. I'll be staying here either way," she added, standing a little taller, even though her insides were trembling. "To defend this place – and myself."

"And I for one won't be leaving her," shouted

Uncle Antoni from the doorway. "That's my niece. You would leave her to face something like that all on her own?"

Lots of people looked at the floor.

"Come on," he said, more gently, in the tone that Nona knew him for. "We've all of us had to fight before, and it's hell. But it's no good giving in now."

"You won't be safe out there," said Serafin. "No one is safe while the Soldier and his rattlesticks walk."

The faces in the crowd looked bewildered. Exhausted and afraid. Fatigue from everything they'd experienced had to be catching up with them. And perhaps they were finally realizing that their ordeal was far from over. All these people had lived through the war, just as Nona had. And Uncle. Most had probably had to fight in it – or treat the injured, or lost loved ones. The last thing any of them would want – the last thing they deserved – was to be asked to endure another battle. Nona understood that.

But what choice was there?

"What do we do?" said someone else. "Just sit around and wait?"

Nona took a deep breath. "What we need to do is finish this building," she said. "Make it as secure as possible. This place was supposed to protect me – but it will protect whoever's in it, I suppose." She glanced at Serafin, who nodded. "Once the magic is sealed not even the Soldier will be able to breach its walls."

An approving murmur went up and a few people started nodding. There was a feeling growing among them all. A feeling of unity. Of strength.

"We have until dawn," she said. "That's when the Soldier plans to attack. The first dawn of the waning moon. It will be a matter of hours." A horrified gasp went up. Quickly Nona added, "But I think we can do it if we work together, fast and non-stop. We *can* do it."

"Perhaps we'll be safe here if we do manage to do all this work," came a single voice in the crowd. "But what happens when we want to leave? I don't want to be stuck here for ever. I've got a family to go back to. And friends. We all have."

Nona's throat tightened. "We'll cross that bridge when we come to it," was all she could offer. But that person, whoever it was, had been right. What would they do once they were safe inside? The rest of the world wouldn't be. And they couldn't stay hidden away for ever. It was an uncomfortable truth that Nona wasn't yet ready for.

Soon there would come a point when Nona either faced the Soldier and won – or failed.

31

EVERYONE SET TO WORK UNDER NONA AND UNCLE Antoni's instruction. Soon there'd be no coming into the church. Or going out.

Much of the final window was in place on the bench, but even so, it would take a lot of effort to finish it. Some glass still needed to be cut and leaded. They still needed the gloopy, black cement – that would stop the glass fragments from rattling around – pushed up underneath the lead with brushes. And then it all had to be cleaned and put into place – either with putty or with wooden trim called beading. And the cement would be wet and runny when they tried to put up the window. Not ideal. Yet at least there was a whole team of tradespeople here who could help. And Serafin had told Nona not to worry – that she would work on a way to help the cement set.

"It's a lot to do," sighed Uncle Antoni. "A good week of work if it was just one person – and we have only until dawn if you're right, Nona. It looks close to midnight to me already. I'd know for certain if only I'd been winding my watch." He had his hands on his hips and his head cocked at a funny angle as he squinted at his own handiwork. Nona repressed a smirk, only to realize that she'd been copying his exact pose. She flushed slightly and turned her attention back to the window.

"We'll need everyone's help," he added. The tone of her uncle's voice made Nona turn towards him, and the look in his eyes made her heart lurch. She understood what he meant. He was asking her to cut the glass.

Nona rarely ever went near the glass itself, being so afraid of it. But now some of that fear ebbed away. Perhaps it was everything that had happened – or knowing that they had to get it finished in time. Either way, she agreed to try.

A couple of times she pressed too hard with the glass cutter and it broke in the wrong direction when she came to put pressure on the glass to make it split. The sound of it splintering set her heart racing and she almost gave up. But soon she got used to listening for the perfect sound as the cutter scored the surface of the glass. She'd heard the sound a million times as Uncle Antoni worked in the studio – and now she heard it made at her own hands: a drawn out *sssshhhhhk*. Like someone soothing a child to sleep, but with a hard note at the very end.

Soon a whole chorus of the *sssshhhhhk* sound was echoing around the hall as a group of them focused on the glass. It soothed Nona. Brought her a sense of peace. This was a controlled cut – not a splintering or a shattering. And although they were breaking the glass, it was in order to put it together again. To make something better.

She was well aware, however, that this calm wouldn't last. She just wasn't expecting it to be shattered so soon.

From the altar came a creak and a yell. Nona dropped her glass cutter and looked up. In the space where the final window would go, a rattlestick leaned through.

It had grabbed hold of one of the tradespeople.

Nona's entire body turned cold.

The rattlestick victim punched it and it fell to bits across the floor. Serafin rushed over to inspect the wound and no doubt heal it. But more rattlesticks had already begun to appear at the window. Nona cried out in horror. There were so many. And it was still dark outside so there'd be yet more to come. What would they do?

"Attack!" shrieked Castor. He bounded across to the window with an armful of stones that he must have summoned the moment the first rattlestick appeared. The bewildered crowd followed his example. With tools and anything else they could find, they rushed to fend off the rattlesticks.

"Don't let them touch you," Nona shouted into the throng.

Uncle Antoni rushed to her. "Nona, stay back here," he said. "We'll handle this."

But Nona's mind whirled in a panic. While they were defending the umbrafell, the window wasn't being built. The Soldier must know that. Her heart sank in despair. It looked hopeless.

But what about Will's matches? If she didn't need him now, when would she? She fumbled in her bag and drew out the box, and with shaking hands she used one to light the nearest of many candles inside the church. The sulphur smell stung the back of her nose as the match flared and lit the wick.

Nona glanced up. In front of her stood Will. He was in his uniform and he seemed younger somehow, and brighter, as though a weight had been lifted from his shoulders. He looked as real as he had done at the lakeside. Even though Nona knew that he couldn't be. Not in the same way that she was real at least. Not any more.

"Will!" Nona flung her arms around him and hugged him hard. He smelled of cold fresh air and stale tobacco. In a rush, Nona told him everything: about the Soldier, the rattlesticks, and that time was running out. Will put one arm around Nona gently.

"You helped me, Nona," he said. "Now allow me and my friends to help you. We can't stay in this world for long, but we'll hold the rattlesticks off for as long as we can to give you all time."

Will looked around at the room. Most people hadn't noticed him appear and were still fighting the rattlesticks at the window with anything they could use. With a smile at Nona, Will walked towards the wall. Just as he reached it, he disappeared.

A gasp went up among those who'd seen it happen. But it was nothing compared to the wave of astonishment that spread among those defending the window. She ran over to look. Squeezing between others at the window, Nona saw what had caused such a huge reaction.

An army of soldiers, translucent in the moonlight, were shoulder to shoulder in a giant ring around the church. They drove forwards, fading to outlines in the moonlight. The rattlesticks were crumbling, some were falling back.

A woman next to Nona wiped sweat from her forehead and sighed deeply. "We're saved," she said.

But Nona felt a twinge of worry. They weren't saved – far from it. They'd just been granted some extra time to work.

While her group cut, Uncle's group leaded, and another soldered as they went. The atmosphere felt more frantic now. The people had seen a glimpse of what they were up against – and Nona could tell it had left them shaken. Once Nona had finished the cutting she felt lost. She paced up and down, desperate to help but not knowing how. Outside a silent battle raged, with nothing but ominous bangs and thumps and thuds to hear. Yet the sound of it made the hairs on her neck stand on end. She had no idea how long Will and his friends could hold off the rattlesticks.

In a flash of inspiration, Nona mixed her flask full of lake water into the cement mix waiting to be pushed under the lead, to strengthen it against any more rattlesticks if they came. But then she was back to feeling lost again, and pacing.

Despite their blip, the final window was coming

together at a rapid pace. It would be plain in terms of detail, but Uncle Antoni's design would make it beautiful no matter what. The window might just be ready before dawn. If they had that long. What more was there for Nona to do? She had to keep busy or she would freeze under the weight of her terror.

She didn't know why. But right then she decided she would paint.

Nona took one diamond-shaped piece from an unassembled part of the panel to work on. She mixed the last drops of the lake water with powdered lead paints and Gum Arabic, which would help it stick when it was heated. This time Serafin, who'd joined Nona for a time, added another ingredient – an adaption of what she planned to use to dry the cement – that would make the paint dry quickly and stick in place without needing a kiln.

For a time, Nona forgot everything else. It was just her and her painting. She worked faster than ever because she didn't want to hold up progress, but she also focused hard.

Finally she sat back in her chair and dropped the paintbrush, her fingers aching.

Uncle Antoni came over and peered over her shoulder. After an agonizing pause he said, "Brilliant work." He wiped his eye and then rested his hand on Nona's shoulder. "Nona, whatever happens here in this place, you will have done us all proud. Especially yourself. Now let's get this piece added to the rest quickly."

Nona's heart soared in her chest as though it had become a wren itself.

The scent of lead and hot tallow hung thick and heavy in the air in a dense fug that reminded Nona of the ever-advancing mist. The fight outside had fallen quiet. Did that mean Will and the ghosts had won, or that they'd done all they could and gone? Nona didn't know, and there was no way to see through that mist. Castor had flown out from the roof to see what he could. But unless he raised the alarm she wouldn't know a thing about how it was going.

And, despite the determination in that place, her thoughts turned more and more to the Soldier. Serafin had told her that if she faced him and was ready, she could win. But would she ever be ready?

Dawn broke as the final stained-glass window went into place. They'd worked all night. Nona surveyed their handiwork with her hands on her hips and a smile on her face: a rainbow hotchpotch of colours. And at the centre, her own panel. She had painted the tree. The one that grew inside the umbrafell. The one that had taken root after the church was destroyed in the human world, and now weaved both worlds together.

She had wanted to tell a story of hope – of life. Of *their* lives. But in the end it was the image of the tree that seemed to capture it all.

Nona looked to Serafin, and Serafin nodded. "Come," she said. "Now for the spell."

Serafin led her to the sapling tree, but Nona hesitated.

"Will this work without Alesea?" she asked. Her voice was hoarse and she felt light-headed after a night awake.

Serafin looked pained, but nodded. "It will," she said. "The magic is already here, contained in this place now. It just needs directing. Take my hand and I'll show you," she added with a smile. "It would be fitting if the person to seal the magic was the one we intended to protect."

Nona took Serafin's hand, closed her eyes and repeated the words Serafin told her.

"*Close these walls to the Soldier and his followers. The ones who would do harm within.*" A surge of warmth travelled through Nona's body and poured out of her chest. When she reopened her eyes a small, pink flower had blossomed on the tree. Nona gasped.

"It is done," Serafin said. "This place will protect us now. The Soldier cannot breach the walls nor step inside."

They had done it. The magic was sealed. In spite of the rattlesticks he'd sent to delay them, the Soldier's belief in the prophesied time had finally been his undoing.

They would be safe.

Again Nona studied the final completed window, her own painted panel. But a movement, a flicker, caught her eye. She peered through the branches, deep into the glass.

Two pairs of eyes looked back at her. Her mother's and her brother's.

Nona caught her breath. They were there for the merest moment. They were together – her brother smiling, her mother with her chin raised in that dignified way of hers. Nona touched the glass where their faces had been. She didn't have time to work out what it meant. But seeing them made her heart swell all the same.

Each of the windows glowed now in the dawn light shining in from outside, a kaleidoscope of lustrous blues, greens and reds. It cast colourful shadows across everything – the benches, the altar, the people.

Nona realized it was the way that the encroaching

white mist affected the light that was making them glow so brilliantly. If she looked closely she could see it touch the glass from outside, twist and curl.

The atmosphere had been charged with a happy defiance. But a sombre air had started to creep into their little bubble. The work was finished. Their focus gone. And the way people wandered around the monument they'd built, it had started to feel uncomfortably like a place of mourning. A tomb – for themselves.

A commotion started up outside. At first Nona wasn't sure what she was hearing. It started as a long harsh shriek, then became a series of short, sharp cries that went on and on.

Castor.

He was raising the alarm.

32

NONA RUSHED UP TO THE ROOF AND POKED HER head through the small hatch. The thick mist hung all around. She searched the billowing whiteness for Castor but found nothing. All she could hear were his ominous cries. They seemed to come from everywhere at once.

A dark shape plunged out of a bank of mist and hurtled through the air. Castor! He arced across the sky like one of his stones. Nona gasped. She couldn't tell if he was flying or falling... Until his wings opened out and he sailed in a full circle around the roof, shrieking and cawing some more.

Something strange was happening to the mist. It looked as if it was retreating. The sky cleared and it sucked itself away over the grass like a reverse wave. As it drew further and further back, skeletal shapes began to emerge from under it. The rattlesticks. Some tall and lean, others hunched over holding torches – and flint daggers – in their hands. Hundreds of them, standing in a crescent shape around the church.

Will and his soldiers were gone, no doubt back to the otherworld. They'd stayed in this world as long as they could. Nona searched the crowd as the mist pulled back further, until her sights settled on the Soldier.

He'd used the mist as cover so they wouldn't be able to see where he approached from – and now he stood tall and proud behind his army of dead things. His skull mask was firmly in place and he looked even taller than before draped in that enormous fur cape. And with those spiked antlers.

No whirlwind whipped around him any more. Though the sky still swirled and roiled with dark clouds. Beneath this layer, the odd pinprick star had come through the dawn sky, violet and blood-red.

Soon they would see if the umbrafell's protective power could stand against the Soldier's.

Something hit Nona in the stomach. When she pulled her head inside she discovered it was Serafin – in owl form – flapping her strong wings. As soon as Nona moved out of the gap, Serafin dived through. She'd wanted to get onto the roof to see what was going on. Nona put her head through the gap again.

The Soldier lifted his head. He looked directly at Nona. Then he raised his arm to point at the umbrafell. The rattlesticks charged towards the building.

"This is it," said Nona to herself. She could barely keep the dread from her voice. "Now we see if the magic works…" Her legs and arms had gone numb and she had to hold onto the hatch to save from collapsing.

Serafin looked at her with blazing orange eyes. Her gaze was steady and firm. Then she turned that gaze on the rattlesticks.

Nona watched too. She held her breath as they drew closer and closer.

Ten paces from the building the rattlesticks leading the charge stopped still. Nona craned her neck to see what was going on. It looked as if they'd frozen. Some staggered a little. Others swayed on the spot. Another wave from behind crashed into them, knocking some over and trampling them underfoot. Then those rattlesticks stopped too…

"It's happening!" Nona bit her lip. "We've done it!" One by one, the rattlesticks at the front began to crumble. Root tore away from stone, until a ring of lifeless debris piled up like driftwood pushed to the shoreline by the tide.

Castor swooped and wheeled overhead, crowing up a storm of his own. On seeing this new wave of rattlesticks fall he seemed to grow bolder. He swooped down closer to those still standing. Taunting them…

Serafin ruffled her feathers. Nona watched with a sick feeling in her throat. Castor needed to be careful.

Nona and Serafin both noticed the rock sail through the air at the same time. It flew as if in slow motion – straight for Castor. And yet it happened so fast. The rock struck Castor hard. He faltered, then righted himself. For one brief second he looked as though he might shake off the blow and keep flying. Then, with a cry that echoed across the moors, he plummeted into the long grass.

The air filled with a series of terrible creaks and clicks. Nona realized it was the rattlesticks straining to see where Castor had landed. Even the Soldier turned his gaze to the patch of grass where the crow had fallen. Nona didn't hesitate.

She felt the transformation before she'd even consciously willed it to happen. It felt like turning herself to paper and scrunching herself up – a tiny, darting ball of feathers: a wren. Before she could fly down there, she heard a familiar voice cry, "Castor!"

The cry came from somewhere close by on the moors. Nona hopped to the edge of the roof and strained to peer over it, but she still couldn't see where the voice came from. That's when she saw a streak of brown and a flash of tail as the hare bounded out of the long grass. It wove between rattlestick bodies and dodged snatching arms to reach Castor, where it transformed into a woman who gathered him to her.

Alesea.

Alesea raised her arm and muttered something Nona couldn't hear. A chasm opened between Alesea and the rattlesticks. It must have taken all her strength – all her remaining magic that hadn't yet been sapped by the Soldier's growing power. Serafin flapped and screeched and swooped towards Alesea. Nona could see now that she had a small pouch in her claws. As Serafin neared she circled above the chasm, dropping herbs from the pouch. A ring of mist rose up, Serafin's this time. It had slowed the rattlesticks down – for now. Some, unable to see in the mist, fell into the maw of the chasm. But others were already edging their way around. And Alesea couldn't drain the rattlesticks the way she could with people. People were alive. The rattlesticks were not.

Nona had to do something to help. If she and Serafin could distract the rattlesticks for long enough, perhaps Alesea and Castor could get inside to safety.

Serafin shrieked once, as if she'd read Nona's mind and agreed with her. Nona felt a chirp bubble up in her own throat from her chest and let it burst from her beak as she took off.

Nona catapulted towards the rattlesticks at top speed. Two saw her coming and stepped back. At the last minute she swerved. Serafin in her eagle owl form was much more menacing. With the protection of her second skin, Serafin raked them with her claws and beat them with her wings, sending their stick bodies scattering. Nona drank it all in. The exhilaration of it. She loved how skilfully she could weave through the air, making last minute twists and turns. She felt unstoppable. Uncatchable. But maybe that was the way Castor had felt... She needed to keep her wits and not get carried away.

With a final spell that made the earth beneath the rattlesticks' feet shudder, Alesea ran for the gap. Nona rose high into the air and did her best dive towards the rattlesticks. She had to keep them distracted until Alesea and Castor were inside. Just a few more seconds. Something small and hard whistled past her – a pebble, most likely. Then another. She dodged them both, but she would have to be careful. So would Serafin. Though she was larger and much more powerful than Nona, she was also slower.

Nona let out a warning cry as she zipped round the ring of rattlesticks, trying to force them back or to fall forwards into the chasm. It had less of an impact this time. They were getting used to her tactics. Serafin screeched in reply and wrenched off a rattlestick arm, then flew high into the air and dropped it. It landed with a clatter on top of several more of the creatures. Alesea and Castor were close enough to the umbrafell to be safe now – at least from the rattlesticks.

But something else was happening. Many of the rattlesticks were turning away from the church. Marching out onto the moors. Had they given up? The Soldier, however, hadn't moved at all.

Nona remained until she saw Alesea and Castor make it safely inside. With a last flourish around the retreating rattlesticks' heads, Nona followed Serafin back inside the roof.

Nona transformed too soon and landed with a crash on the floor. Serafin, on the other hand, transformed gracefully in mid-air and landed on her feet.

"Now what?" said Nona, breathless from the fall.

"Now you all stay inside where it's safe," answered Serafin. "I have to go."

"What?" Nona stared at her in disbelief from the floor. "Why can't you stay? Out there you'll…"

"I can't just give up on every other person alive out there," said Serafin. Her jaw was set. "You've saved the people here, Nona, and you should be proud. We've made the prophecy he saw happen on the dawn of the waning moon impossible. But until

you're ready to face him the fight goes on elsewhere."
Serafin turned and walked towards the hatch. Any
second now she would transform and be gone. And
that might be the last Nona would ever see of her.
The thought wrenched her stomach. She'd grown to
love Serafin.

"Wait!" Nona clambered back onto her feet and
ran to Serafin. It was hard to even walk straight – she
felt wobbly after all that flying. "This can't just be it."

Serafin paused but didn't turn around again. "I'm
afraid it is, Nona. You've done your best. Now you
must keep safe. I will visit, if I can."

Nona couldn't believe it. This was it? Nona had
trapped *herself*? Maybe she had helped save all those
who now huddled inside. But what Serafin had said
was true. While she was safe in here, the rest of the
world would suffer.

Unless she faced the Soldier – and won.

A thought struck her so hard that it sent her
wobbling on her feet again. Nona gasped. They'd
trapped themselves inside the umbrafell. But what
if she could trap the Soldier inside instead? Nona's
mouth dropped open and her whole body tingled as
another thought – a more frightening one – crept into
her mind and made her skin prickle. With everyone
safely outside except for her and the Soldier, and him

cut off from his rattlesticks, perhaps she could even find a way to stop him for good ... although she would keep that thought to herself. Serafin and Alesea would never agree that she was ready. And maybe she wasn't. But she wouldn't know unless she tried.

"Serafin, stop," she said. "I've had an idea. I might just have a way to stop the Soldier."

33

SHOUTING CAME FROM THE STAIRS. UNCLE ANTONI and the tradesman had clearly tried to run up the stairs at the same time and got themselves stuck shoulder to shoulder.

"Hey! What are you doing to my roof?" shouted the tradesman.

Uncle Antoni barged in front of him. "Nona? Are you all right?"

"I'm fine, Uncle," she said. They hugged, then Nona and Serafin rushed down the stairs. Alesea sat at the centre of the umbrafell with Castor – an imp – on her knee. Apart from being a little dazed he looked OK. As Alesea stroked his scales they shimmered gold.

Nona let out a sigh of relief. Castor looked up, grinned, and bounded over to her. They hugged.

When Nona looked back at Alesea, she found her looking grave.

"I'm sorry," Alesea said in a choked voice. "To all of you." She looked at Castor, and then at Serafin. "Especially to you, sister. And, Castor, my darling. For running away and leaving you to deal with all this. For everything. I abandoned you."

"But you came through for Castor," said Nona, crossing the room to rest her hand on Alesea's shoulder. "That must have taken a lot."

Alesea flushed and smiled slightly – a true one. Serafin approached too and rested her hand on Alesea's other shoulder.

"We can talk about this later. But you're here now," she said simply.

Serafin was right: there was no time to chat. Nona had to tell them her plan – to lure the Soldier into the umbrafell and seal him inside.

Once Nona had explained everything, Serafin's eyes sparkled. "Of course," she said. "It's *brilliant*. If it works." Worry clouded her expression in an instant.

Nona could see from her face – from all of their faces – that this was a huge risk. They had built this place to protect whoever was inside. She'd promised it would keep them all safe... And now Nona was proposing they abandon it. All for the tiny chance that she could bring the Soldier inside. Trap him there. And if Serafin was looking worried, it had to be a dangerous idea. If something went wrong and Nona got caught...

Serafin took Nona's face in her hand firmly. "You'll need our help," she said. "I'll come with you. Alesea will evacuate the others."

"Listen to Serafin, Jenny Wren," said Uncle Antoni, his face a sea of worry. "At least have her with you, in case anything happens."

Castor cawed and bobbed his head again.

"No." It was hard looking into Serafin's stern face and disagreeing with her. But she had to. To Uncle Antoni she said, "I'm smallest – and quickest. I have the best chance of luring the Soldier inside and escaping. It's me he wants – to bring back his son. Serafin, you and Alesea need to work together to protect the others during the evacuation."

Serafin chewed her lip in agitation and looked at Alesea. Alesea looked back. Who knew what the Soldier was up to outside – what he might be planning next? They had to do something. A thin smile crept across Serafin's face.

Without taking her eyes off Alesea, Serafin nodded. "All right," she said to Nona. "But if you fail, it doesn't matter where we take them. He'll take his wrath out on them all. Not just on Alesea. Or me."

"I know." Nona fought down the terror that kept rising up. "But this is the only way to stop him for good."

"And, Nona, the moment he's in the umbrafell, you are to escape. Don't risk anything." Again, Serafin had an uncanny way of guessing what she was thinking. Murmurs of agreement went up among them all, and Nona squirmed under their gaze. She hadn't told anyone about her plan to face the Soldier once they were alone and given the chance.

"I promise," she said, hoping the lie didn't tell on her face.

"I'm coming too," crowed Castor. He flew from Alesea's shoulder and onto Nona's. She opened her mouth to tell him that he couldn't – that he was hurt and he had to rest. But she already knew he would be too stubborn to listen.

"All right," she said. "You can keep the rest of the rattlesticks busy while I deal with the Soldier. Deal? And, Castor. I need you to do something else. To wait for me by the door and help me bar it shut with the Soldier inside – once I make it out. I'll have to undo the spell to let him in and then put it back on before I escape. Shutting the door will seal the magic properly and trap him."

Castor squawked so loudly it made them all wince, and the workman cover his ears. He took off and landed on the hatch, one-footed, and squawked again.

"All right, all right! I'm coming," said Nona. "And you," she said, turning to the workman they'd first met in the roof. "You'll need to barricade the hatch once we're gone. To block off all escape routes for the Soldier. Use anything you've got. And leave behind something for us next to the door, so we can nail it shut."

The man's eyebrows looked like they were trying to join forces with the hair on his head. But he nodded. Nona's throat was dry and her stomach churned. She couldn't back out now.

Castor took off from the hatch without a second's thought. Serafin gave the back of Nona's neck a tight squeeze. "We'll do our best not to let you down," she said.

Nona smiled. "I know. Thank you."

It didn't take long to undo the spell that kept the Soldier outside. Nona just closed her eyes and reversed the words. "Open these walls to the Soldier. The one who would do harm within," she whispered. Even as she said it she fretted that she'd made a huge mistake – but there was no time to reconsider.

She felt no flood of warmth this time – just a creeping coldness that made her shudder. When she opened her eyes the tree's small pink blossom had wilted away and fallen.

Nona rushed back to the roof, and hugged Uncle Antoni. But when she pulled back his face wore a frown. "*Mój Boże.* Nona, Listen." As she looked into his worried eyes, she found that she was holding her breath.

"If there's anything I've learned from flying in the war, it's this," he said. "You and Castor must work as a team. Look out for each other, work together. Height gives you the advantage. *Don't* glide at one level for too long – that's what got Castor knocked down. Go in quickly, do what you must do, and get straight out."

This was the first time he'd spoken to her properly about the war. His eyes were red-rimmed, his face pale. All Nona could do was nod furiously, squeeze his arms tight.

"Stay safe," he said as he stroked her hair. "Please. Remember what I've told you."

"I'll try." And with that, Nona became a wren once more, and zipped out of the hatch after Castor.

Many of the rattlesticks had scattered by the time she emerged into the evening air. But the Soldier remained.

Castor was already swooping and reeling at the rattlesticks. He'd done a great job; they were fully distracted by him. Nona could only hope that this time he would be more wary of hurled stones.

Nona landed right in front of the Soldier and transformed into her human self.

The Soldier turned his skull-covered head towards her. He stared at her through the dark hollows of the eyes. Nona took a deep breath.

"I came to speak with you, to try to convince you to let your grudge go." Her voice trembled as she spoke, but she kept going. "You didn't listen. So now I've come to stop you – for good."

A sound boomed from beneath the skull – a cold, mocking laugh. Its joylessness sent shivers through Nona's body. The Soldier raised an arm and removed the skull that covered his face. His skin was bone white and the rims of his eyes blood red. He had a scratch on his face that hung open. But there was no blood to be seen in the wound. No scab or scar had formed. From beneath his dark clothes his sorcerer's glass heart glowed.

"Here she is. The sacrifice," he said. His voice was deep, but clear as a bell. The sound of it seemed to travel through her whole body. There was something hypnotic – persuasive – to its tone. "Come closer, little mouse," he said. "It will be over quickly."

Nona knew she mustn't listen. She had to think clearly. Stick to the plan – at least, her version of it. She pushed her fear down, out of her thoughts.

"I'll be your sacrifice if you can catch me," said Nona, glancing at Castor, who was keeping the rattlesticks busy, and then back at the umbrafell. She could just about see the sliver of the open door. They must be watching from behind it. Waiting until the Soldier wasn't looking, so they could make their escape to one of the nearby houses. Nona felt a twinge of relief. It was all working so far. "But I won't make it easy."

Nona became a wren again and zipped around the Soldier's head. His arm swiped past. It just missed her. The pulse of air it sent out, however, knocked her off course. She dipped, but quickly righted herself, and put distance between them. She would take the Soldier around the umbrafell – away from the doors at first – giving everyone inside a chance to escape. And then she would lead him inside.

Another arm swiped the air beside her. This time she felt a claw come close to catching her wing. She didn't understand it. How had he managed to reach her when she'd gained so much height? And how had he been so fast? Nona flitted round to look.

Just in time to see the Soldier halfway through a transformation. His fur cloak had gathered in around his body to create a huge fur torso. His face elongated into that of a bear's. But there was something different about this transformation. As she watched, his body changed shape again. His head extended into a long neck, the stag skull atop it – and the arm he'd swiped at her with became the talons of an unnaturally giant eagle.

Was this all the power contained within his glass heart? Panic swelled in her chest. How could she possibly defeat him? Hopes to lure him inside the umbrafell and fight him now felt ridiculous.

But Nona didn't waste time. She mustn't think about it or she'd lose her focus completely. She flew as fast as she could around the back of the umbrafell, turning only once to make sure the Soldier was following. When she did, she got a fright.

He no longer resembled a man at all – or any one kind of animal. He towered as high as the church roof on four strange, ever-changing stilt-like legs, so that his face – the skull mask – was always level with her. One front arm became a hook – like that of a sloth – which he used to swipe at her again. Even though he missed Nona, the shockwaves it sent out almost knocked her from the air. Deep inside the swirling storm of his body hung the red glass heart, from which a wisp of black smoke leaked from the tiniest trace of a crack.

All she had to do was keep it up a little bit longer. She just had to last long enough to lead him inside…

The Soldier roared – a guttural, animal sound that shook the earth. Like a horse, and a bear, and some ancient prehistoric raptor, all rolled into one. They were on the opposite side to the door of the church now. Nona risked gaining height to glance over the top, and caught sight of a line of people streaming from the door. Serafin, Alesea and Uncle Antoni were guiding them towards one of the nearest cottages. If she could keep the Soldier busy for a few moments more, they'd all be safe.

Nona looped in a circle, momentarily dizzying herself. She saw the Soldier upside down – the skull resting on top of a giant, deformed crocodile-like mouth. Its jaws snapped at her, catching one wing and sending up a plume of feathers. Nona plummeted towards the floor. For a moment, she couldn't remember how to fly. Being a human and a wren was a jumble inside her panicked head. Her wings felt stuck to her sides.

She prised them away from her body just before she hit the earth. She glided above the ground, the grass whipping past. To her right, the Soldier brought down a giant claw aimed for Nona – bear-like again – which scraped a huge crater out of the earth right next to her.

From the church roof, Castor cawed.

Had the people finally made it out?

To her relief, she saw the end of the trail of people disappearing inside the cottage. No more delaying. Now to lead the Soldier inside.

The Soldier's jaws snapped again. Every bone in Nona's bird body ached with the effort of flying, but she drove herself on with renewed determination. She whisked around the side of the umbrafell as fast as she could and raced around to the next corner. There was the door, right in front of her and getting closer. They'd left it wide open for her – along with the wood, hammer and nails she and Castor would need to seal it up once she'd hopefully escaped.

Another roar blasted her from behind. He was so close she could feel the hot, rank-smelling wind made by his breath. She plunged through the doors, transformed, and skidded to a halt in the aisle as a human.

Nona held her breath, watched the doors, and

waited. She shuddered. There was no going back. If she saw any chance to defeat the Soldier for good once they were alone, she would take it. If not, she would simply reinvoke the spell asking the walls to protect them. Surely it would still work, even with him on the inside and them on the outside... And then – by sealing the Soldier inside – they would be free.

The giant sloth-claw hooked around the door. The claws were as long as the door itself, and the colour of opaque quartz that was engrained with dirt. For a moment she wondered how he would fit inside. Or if he would realize her plan. Then something dark and as fluid as cloud pushed through, carrying with it the skull on top. It looked tiny now, in comparison with the rest of him. As if it was floating on the swell of floodwater.

It was definitely him. The Soldier. And he was coming in. The walls of the umbrafell groaned, as if crying out in dismay.

His body was more like a shifting mass of energy than anything else. One that couldn't decide what it was. That could be anything at all. Slowly, the rest of him slithered in, like smoke. Until he filled the entire far end of the church, right up to the ceiling. Still at the centre hung the red glass heart, the smoke flooding out of it like poison. If only she could get to the heart...

Nona glanced around. How could she get close enough? What could she use to attack it? Diamond could cut glass, but lots of other things could smash it. Would only magic destroy magic though? *Of course.* The Soldier had shattered her half-heart but she'd hung onto one single shard. Perhaps her glass was exactly what would destroy the heart.

She hoped Castor was waiting by the door as they'd agreed. If this all went wrong, if he saw her glass and snatched it, Castor would still need to seal the door shut.

Nona shuffled back across the floor – further and further towards the sapling. Her trembling hand went to her pocket, found the fragment and began to unwrap it. The Soldier followed her – his arms creeping forwards like a stalking cat, while his body wound and coiled like a giant snake.

The protective power of this place did seem to be doing *something* to him… Every time his cloud-like body touched the windows, it withdrew as though stung, or burned. Momentarily making him shrink.

As the body towered over her, the glass heart hovered closer.

"You thought you could defeat me in here, didn't you?" The Soldier's voice rumbled around the room. It rattled the windows, making Nona wince. "I'm not as naïve as your friends, little mouse. I know a tactic of war when I see one. But you've given up your only sanctuary – and I've still caught you. A childish mistake."

Still edging towards the sapling, Nona finished unwrapping the glass shard. Her finger grazed the sharp edge. It cut – and stung. She gritted her teeth and focused on the Soldier. On allowing him to get close enough that she could get nearer to the heart.

He stalked closer and closer as he spoke, his body more like a dragon's now. The Soldier, for all his wiles, hadn't realized he'd been brought into a trap. She must either attack or be imprisoned along with him.

"I'm sorry about your son," said Nona, slowly edging round. "But I won't give up my life. That's not something I'll let you take." Still concealed in her pocket, Nona gripped the base of the dagger-like glass shard. She had her back to the young sapling growing through the centre of the umbrafell now. The very last piece of the Soldier's tail whipped in through the door.

That was it. She'd led him in far enough.

With her other hand against the sapling's slender trunk, she whispered the incantation. *"Close these walls to the Soldier and his followers. The ones who would do harm within."* She hoped against hope that it would work the way she wanted it to – trap him inside. Before it had been different, but now she felt anything but confident. She felt no warmth, and didn't dare take her eyes from the Soldier to check the tree for any more telltale blossoms.

A long slit opened up in the Soldier's body, like a giant mouth – and bared its teeth. A deep growl emanated from the heart exposed within.

"Nowhere to run now, little mouse. I can't be harmed." The Soldier seemed to grow in size, filling the whole hall. His whip-like tail slammed the door shut. Her only escape route, gone. There was only one thing for it. To attack. Was it her only means of escape, though? There was the sapling. Perhaps she could move through it? It might not be possible. But it was her only option.

The giant mouth bore down on her. As did the heart.

Nona pulled the glass dagger from her pocket and plunged it straight into the heart as hard as she could. The heart splintered. Exploded into shards.

Nona didn't wait to see what happened. She whipped round and placed her hand against the sapling tree. *Let me through to the hidden path*, she said in her head. Beneath her hands, the tree split apart, opened wide, and she stepped inside.

Behind her, the Soldier roared. But Nona was

inside. The tree sealed behind her, and all she could hear was the rushing of wind as she ran through what felt like nothing at all.

And then she part ran, part fell from one of the old graves in the church grounds, outside in the cold, crisp night air once more.

"Quick, Castor," yelled Nona. "The door." Although she was sure the Soldier was defeated, she wasn't taking any chances. Castor cried out in relief when he saw her, but wheeled round instantly and charged towards the door. Others were there too – Serafin, Alesea, Uncle Antoni and more. They must have come when they heard Castor's distress. They caught on straight away and braced the door with all their might.

Nona ran to help them. The door rattled on its hinges, but once shut, it seemed to seal the magic fully – because it took little effort for them to hold it closed.

"What took you so long?" asked Serafin.

"The heart," gasped Nona, still breathless. "I shattered it."

Alesea and Serafin stared at her. Castor squawked and flapped. Uncle Antoni looked like he might pass out. Inside, the raging of the Soldier boomed. His shifting smoke-like body filled the building, pulling away the moment it touched the glass, the walls, all imbued with protective magic.

As soon as they had nailed the planks in place, they stepped back from the door.

"Have you really done it, Nona?" gasped Alesea. She took Nona's hand in hers. "Have you really defeated the Soldier?"

Serafin, over her shoulder, smiled. "It looks like she has, sister. Oh, for the wiles of a human."

Nona collapsed onto the grass, exhausted. It was over. It really was.

34

THE PARTY LASTED FOR DAYS. THEIR DEFEAT OF THE Soldier had given everyone renewed energy. Despite their previous exhaustion, they wouldn't have been able to sleep now if they'd tried.

They ate honey brought to them by Alesea, sang songs together from the hilltops, and danced barefoot with her through the moors. Even Serafin gave up insisting that she needed to get home because she had things to do, and eventually let her hair down with the others. She didn't have to deal with any more rattlesticks, after all. And secretly, Nona thought, she seemed to be enjoying the companionship of all these people.

Soon the full force of everything she'd had to face caught up with Nona. The fear of almost losing her uncle. The exhaustion of building the umbrafell's final window. The terror of facing the Soldier. It crashed on top of her in wave upon wave, until the warmth and the din of the party felt to her like drowning. She slipped out onto the cool of the moors, gasping for air, and rested her back against the stone wall of one of the cottages. She let her gaze take it all in: the sky. The valleys. The hills. And, inevitably, the umbrafell.

There, with his back propped against a gravestone that stood in the grounds, sat an old man, dressed all in black.

Nona's heart leaped into her mouth. It was the Soldier. It had to be. *How* had he survived? How had he escaped? Nona pressed against the wall and held her breath, wondering what she should do. Run back inside and raise the alarm? Become a wren and lead him away? But as she watched, the Soldier didn't move. He just sat there, his arms resting on his knees, staring out at the horizon, as though lost deep in thought. Nona relaxed a little. Enough to peel herself away from the wall.

Bit by bit, Nona crept towards the old man. The closer she got, the more she noticed about him. He still wore his black fur cape around his shoulders – but didn't have the skull he'd worn as a mask. He looked a great deal smaller. There was something about him now – a feeling – that reminded Nona of Will.

The umbrafell's magic would not have let him leave if he still intended harm. And if he was a ghost … surely he could no longer do harm, even if he tried.

Still he didn't look up. Even when she came right up beside him.

In spite of her trembling, Nona was intent on being brave. In a loud voice she said, "How did you get out?"

The Soldier laughed weakly. "I don't even know how I came to be here, little one. Let alone anything else." Then he said, as though just remembering, "I had a child like you, once. A boy. Yes, that's right. A son." Nona didn't say anything, but stood, watching him. His voice wasn't the clear, deep boom it had once been – but the crackle of an elderly man's. He couldn't have been that old, considering he'd been little more than a teenager in the Great War. But perhaps his sorcery – his glass heart – which had once promised to prolong his life, had aged him. He spoke as if he didn't know Nona at all – or what he'd become.

The old man shifted his body to look at her for the first time. He grimaced with the effort. "You know," he said, looking her in the eye, "you remind me very much of my son. But perhaps it's just because you're young. He's gone, of course. He died years ago. My precious boy."

"You look tired," said Nona, stepping closer. All her fear of him was gone. She knew what she ought to do. Just as she had done at the lakeside with Will.

Nona felt her neck prickle and spun around. Alesea stood some way off, frozen to the spot. She was watching them. She gave Nona the smallest smile, and a nod. Nona turned back to the Soldier.

"Maybe … maybe I can help you to be with him again," she said. "Would you like that?"

The Soldier smiled. "Oh, yes," he said. "Nothing would make me happier."

"Then rest." Nona put her hand on the Soldier's shoulder. Her fingers sank into the black fur of his cape. Instantly she felt the power spilling from her chest, working its way down her arm, into her hand, and through him. The way it had done with Will. It brought tears to her eyes, to think of him. "You can go now," she said.

The Soldier let out a long sigh. Thunder rumbled overhead. The old man's outline blurred, drifted, and disappeared – like smoke. He had evaporated like a spent storm.

The men and women who'd been inside the church had started fires for warmth and still chatted and laughed together. Uncle Antoni was sound asleep with rosy cheeks and a smile on his face. No one had noticed Nona slip out or return.

Nona found Serafin watching the celebrations from a distance. "What will you do now?" she asked quietly.

"Me? Oh, I'll find something to keep me busy. Don't you worry about that. Alesea and I intend to continue with our work now that we no longer have the Soldier to fret about – or those tiresome rattlesticks. But it would be nice to see some of our friends again. And it might even keep her out of trouble for a while." Serafin grinned in a way Nona had never seen her do before, and Nona couldn't help but laugh.

Later, she wandered outside and sat on the grass by herself again, musing over everything that had happened. She couldn't take her eyes off the umbrafell. It was hard to believe everything that had taken place there. She was so deep in thought that it took her by surprise when Castor landed on her shoulder with a *thud*.

"*Craaw*," he said, but his tone was mournful. Perhaps he'd had enough of the party too.

"What will you do now, Castor?" she asked. "Will you stay, do you think?" This had been his home until they came along. But it had changed beyond all recognition.

Castor transformed into an imp and swished his tail. "Suppose I'll stay," he said. "I managed here on my own for all these years. Well – with Alesea. I can keep on managing a bit longer." Nona thought he sounded sad.

She didn't want to leave Castor behind. "Why don't you come with us?" she said suddenly. "Me and Uncle Antoni. You'd be welcome, I promise! Uncle Antoni would definitely say yes."

"Well, Castor? Would you like to?" came a voice from behind. Nona twisted round. Alesea stood there, clutching her hands in front of her, her eyebrows knitted together. Castor looked between her and Nona. Alesea spoke again. "Would you like to go with Nona and her uncle? If that's what would make you happy, my boy, you'd be free to."

Castor's grip on Nona's shoulder tightened with excitement. Then worry troubled his face. His scales didn't know what colour to be – turning blue and green and purple. "What about you, Alesea?" he said. "I can't leave you…"

Alesea grinned. "Oh, don't worry about me. I'll be with Serafin," she said, "and when I miss you or you miss me I can visit, can't I?"

Castor hesitated. Then, in two bounds, he leaped off Nona's shoulder and into Alesea's arms. The two embraced tightly.

"My Castor," Alesea said, sniffing. "I do love you, darling, and I always will." Castor didn't reply – only hugged Alesea as tightly as his arms could manage.

Alesea set Castor on the ground and straightened. "Now," she said. "How to make you human again, Castor, if that's what would really make you happy. I know you and Serafin have tried, but if she and I put our heads together we can surely find a way."

"Nah," said Castor, scuffing the ground. The shine came off his scales in an instant and he turned a deep, dull grey. "I'm an imp. Always have been, always will be. If Serafin's potion had worked, it would've shown by now, but it hasn't. I've just got to live with it, I suppose."

"That's not true." Nona bent down next to him and looked him in the eye. "Castor, you're a human being. I've seen you. I know." She remembered how he'd looked through the half-heart glass. How perfect in imperfectness he'd been. The glass was gone now – shattered into shards. But Nona's memory of what she'd glimpsed in it remained – more a feeling than an image. At the time she'd wanted more than anything to show him what she'd seen, so that he would understand his true self. Perhaps she could still show him?

She reached out and placed her hand on Castor's shoulder. The heat in her chest was instant. It sparked down her arm and through her fingers. Castor's eyes widened in amazement as he felt it.

As she stared into his deep blue eyes, the face around them started to change. She was *sure* of it. It started off slow, but soon there was no denying it. Until Nona was no longer staring into the face of an imp.

But of a boy.

35

Nona stared out of the van window as the moors retreated from view. Finally, they were going home to the workshop. Her, Uncle Antoni and Castor.

"*Craaw,*" Castor said, perched on the head rest of the seat between Nona and Uncle Antoni. He'd been forbidden from flying in the car, and he seemed happy enough to abide by that rule – for now. He might have got his human form back, but it didn't stop him from enjoying his second skin. Uncle Antoni hummed to himself softly as he drove.

Nona smiled and wiped the mist of her breath from the window.

All of a sudden, Uncle Antoni stopped humming. "Nona?" he said. The sound of his voice made Nona tense her shoulders and turn around. He sounded anxious – the same way his eyes looked when she saw them.

"What is it, Uncle?" she asked. Her heart skipped a little faster. "Are you feeling all right?"

"Oh, I'm fine," he said with a grin. "Fine. It's just…" His tone changed, as did his expression. "If there's anything about what happened – these past days, or even, er … before we met, that you would like to talk about…" Uncle Antoni rubbed the back of his neck and turned back towards the road.

"I used to think that some things were too big to discuss," he went on quietly. "And, if I'm honest, that it was a terrible burden to other people to hear them. I thought the only thing for it was to leave it in the past where it belongs. But now I'm not sure it gets left behind at all." He cleared his throat. This was obviously hard for him to say. "Perhaps sharing what you can, with someone you trust, in whatever way you choose, can make it lighter for a time."

Castor watched them in silence with his head cocked. Nona reached out and squeezed Uncle Antoni's arm. "Thank you, Uncle," she said.

During their celebrations, after the Soldier was trapped, she'd seen him speaking with Serafin and Alesea, seen them both listening with serious frowns. Alesea with her hand on his shoulder, Serafin with her hand in his. What they'd talked about she might never know – but she suspected it was all the things that he could never say to her. About his war.

She'd realized something else too. About Uncle Antoni's artwork, and what made him a master. Whether he knew it or not, he put all of himself into it. Just as she did. Both the darkness and the light.

❧❧❧❧❧

The studio felt cold when Nona stepped inside – but never more like home. Uncle Antoni was still sorting out their things from the back of the van, with Castor on his shoulder. The air was still, and the warm smell of linseed oil, the dapple of colours splaying across the stairs, all felt like a part of herself she'd forgotten about until now. She was glad to get them back.

That night Nona couldn't sleep. She lit a candle at her drawing desk and sat down at the page. Outside the foxes howled and the river ran. Inside the house, all was quiet.

By the flickering candlelight, the glass of her bedroom window glowed brilliantly. She stared deeply into it, beyond the light dancing across its surface. Into the shadows of the outside world. Beyond even that.

She found herself staring at the figure of a young man, little more than a silhouette on the horizon.

He wore a cape that twisted, smoke like, around his ankles. At his side stood a much smaller figure – a boy. As she watched, both of them raised an arm – a wave, or an officer's salute, Nona couldn't tell. Barely had she blinked when both of them faded and were gone.

Acknowledgements

Firstly, thank you to Bryony Woods for being the best agent and champion of my writing that I could ever have hoped for.

I'm so grateful to everyone at Walker, and by extension all who worked on this book, whose many contributions have created *Glassheart*. Particularly Annalie Grainger for getting the ball rolling, Denise Johnstone-Burt and Megan Middleton for putting their all into helping me get *Glassheart* into shape, and Rebecca Oram and the whole marketing team for championing it. Ben Norland and Sandra Dieckmann, what an incredible cover you've created!

Thank you, James Combes, for posting paracetamol through the letterbox during lockdown when I was poorly and redrafting. And to Lucy Axon, my parents, and neighbours Sally, Justin and Alicia for similar acts of kindness – Sally for the Dartmoor information too.

Every friend, family member or well-wisher who

shared my excitement when *Nevertell* was released and has been so supportive and enthusiastic ever since – **you know who you are** and thank you so much. That includes all the teachers, librarians, booksellers, bloggers and more who spread the word about *Nevertell*, and fans who got in touch to tell me they loved it. I hope you love *Glassheart* too! To my local Bristol bookshop, Storysmith: you're awesome. To new author friends, too, for your support and camaraderie, and all my former colleagues at the Creative Glass Guild for the glassy knowledge and fun.

Much love to my mum, dad and all the Ortons and Axons, Jon (one man sales team), Jane and the Pullaras, and Lin, Rob and the Wildings. Matt and Isaac Pullara, my own little family, thank you both for the immeasurable and enduring love and support. Isaac, I enjoyed our covert whispers about what was going to happen next in the book.

Lastly, I'd like to pay tribute to my grandparents – Jack and Sadie Orton, and Nan and Keith Axon – who each had their own very different experiences of war. Nan, who was my last living grandparent, died while I was writing the first draft of this book, and it was her story about listening to an air raid overhead on the night before being evacuated to Australia that first seeded the idea of the Soldier. This book is for Nan, and all of us who miss her.

After gaining an English degree and an MA
in creative writing, KATHARINE ORTON worked
for Barefoot Books in Bath before leaving to focus
on her writing and her young family. She signed
with her agent after taking part in the brilliant
WoMentoring Project. Katharine's debut, *Nevertell*,
was published in 2019 to critical acclaim; *Glassheart*
is her second novel. She currently lives in Bristol.